THE THEBAN PLAYS

Oedipus Rex, Oedipus at Colonus, and Antigone

DOVER THRIFT EDITIONS

Sophocles
Translated by Sir George Young

DOVER PUBLICATIONS, INC.
MINEOLA, NEW YORK

DOVER THRIFT EDITIONS

GENERAL EDITOR: MARY CAROLYN WALDREP
EDITOR OF THIS VOLUME: T. N. R. ROGERS

Theatrical Rights

This Dover Thrift Edition may be used in its entirety, in adaptation, or in any other way for theatrical productions, professional and amateur, in the United States, without fee, permission, or acknowledgment. (This may not apply outside of the United States, as copyright conditions may vary.)

Bibliographical Note

This Dover edition, first published in 2006, contains the unabridged republication of the plays *Oedipus Tyrannus*, *Oedipus Coloneus*, and *Antigone* from the volume *The Dramas of Sophocles Rendered in English Verse Dramatic & Lyric by Sir George Young*, as published by J. M. Dent & Sons, Ltd., London, in 1906. (The Dent edition was the second; the first edition was published by George Bell & Sons, London, in 1888.) The first of these plays was republished as *Oedipus Rex* in a 1991 Dover Thrift Edition; the second as *Oedipus at Colonus* in a 1999 Dover Thrift Edition; and the third, *Antigone*, in a 1993 Dover Thrift Edition. Brief introductory Notes and a few footnotes were written specially for the Dover editions. Sir George's original footnotes have been omitted.

Library of Congress Cataloging-in-Publication Data

Sophocles.
  [Selections. English. 2006]
  The Theban plays / Sophocles ; translated by Sir George Young.
     p. cm. — (Dover thrift editions)
  ISBN-13: 978-0-486-45049-0
  ISBN-10: 0-486-45049-X
  1. Sophocles—Translations into English. 2. Oedipus (Greek mythology)—Drama. 3. Antigone (Greek mythology)—Drama. I. Young, George, Sir, 1837–1930. II. Title. III. Series.

PA4414.A2Y68 2006
882'.01—dc22

                                                          2006041118

Manufactured in the United States by LSC Communications
45049X10   2020
www.doverpublications.com

Note

SOPHOCLES (born ca. 496 B.C., died after 413) was one of the three major authors of Greek tragedy. He wrote some 123 plays, only seven of which survive in full. These works brought him extraordinary acclaim in his day, for in the annual Dionysian festival they never won less than second place, and they captured first place twenty times.

The three plays included here, sometimes called the Theban or Cadmean Trilogy, were written over a forty-year period (and not in order of dramatic chronology). They contradict each other frequently. It has been noted, for instance, that the character of Creon is wildly different from play to play; that circumstances presented at the close of *Oedipus the King* are overlooked or radically changed at the outset of *Oedipus at Colonus*, and so on. Therefore, although it is quite possible to learn interesting things by comparing them, it is widely agreed that the three should be considered separate dramatic entries.

The translations by Sir George Young (1837–1930) reprinted here are not only very accurate; they also preserve the feeling of the original Greek to a great extent. The verse forms are reasonable English equivalents; the diction — lightly archaic in the blank-verse dialogues, heightened and more complex in the stanzaic choruses — admirably reflects the hieratic nature of Sophocles' drama.

In the present edition, Sir George's own notes (exclusively concerned with problems of the Greek text and its interpretation) have been omitted. Several new, very brief footnotes have been added, identifying references to places or deities with which the reader may not be familiar; when they may be found in standard reference works, unfamiliar references have not been footnoted.

Contents

Oedipus Rex   1

Oedipus at Colonus   57

Antigone   115

Oedipus Rex

We are fortunate that one of Sophocles' surviving plays is *Oedipus Rex* (in Greek, *Oidipous tyrannos*), written soon after 430 B.C., which the ancient Greeks themselves considered his best work.

Still exciting to read or see, *Oedipus Rex* is famous for its smooth and suspenseful plotting, its cosmic ironies, and the philosophical questions it raises about the limits of man's power and ambitions. (Note: *Antigone*, *Oedipus Rex*, and *Oedipus at Colonus* were written many years apart, and do not form a trilogy.)

STANLEY APPELBAUM

Persons Represented

OEDIPUS, *King of Thebes.*

PRIEST *of Zeus.*

CREON, *brother to Jocasta the Queen.*

TIRESIAS, *a Prophet, with the title of King.*

A Messenger from Corinth.

An old Shepherd.

A Second Messenger, servant of Oedipus' household.

JOCASTA *the Queen, wife to Oedipus, formerly married to Laius, the last King.*

ANTIGONE, } *daughters to Oedipus and Jocasta.*
ISMENE,

The CHORUS *is composed of Senators of Thebes.*

Inhabitants of Thebes, Attendants.

A Boy leading Tiresias.

Oedipus Rex

Scene, before the Royal Palace at Thebes. Enter OEDIPUS; *to him the Priest of Zeus, and Inhabitants of Thebes.*

OEDIPUS   Children, you modern brood of Cadmus* old,
    What mean you, sitting in your sessions here,
    High-coronalled with votive olive-boughs,
    While the whole city teems with incense-smoke,
    And paean hymns, and sounds of woe the while?
    Deeming unmeet, my children, this to learn
    From others, by the mouth of messengers,
    I have myself come hither, Oedipus,
    Known far and wide by name. Do thou, old man,
    Since 'tis thy privilege to speak for these,
    Say in what case ye stand; if of alarm,
    Or satisfaction with my readiness
    To afford all aid; hard-hearted must I be,
    Did I not pity such petitioners.

PRIEST   Great Oedipus, my country's governor,
    Thou seest our generations, who besiege
    Thy altars here; some not yet strong enough
    To flutter far; some priests, with weight of years
    Heavy, myself of Zeus; and these, the flower
    Of our young manhood; all the other folk
    Sit, with like branches, in the market-place,

* Founder of Thebes.

By the Ismenian hearth oracular*
And the twin shrines of Pallas.** Lo, the city
Labours—thyself art witness—over-deep
Already, powerless to uprear her head
Out of the abysses of a surge of blood;
Stricken in the budding harvest of her soil,
Stricken in her pastured herds, and barren travail
Of women; and He, the God with spear of fire,
Leaps on the city, a cruel pestilence,
And harries it; whereby the Cadmean home
Is all dispeopled, and with groan and wail
The blackness of the Grave made opulent.
Not that we count thee as the peer of Heaven,
I, nor these children, seat us at thy hearth;
But as of men found foremost in affairs,
Chances of life and shifts of Providence;
Whose coming to our Cadmean town released
The toll we paid, of a hard Sorceress,***
And that, without instruction or advice
Of our imparting; but of Heaven it came
Thou art named, and known, our life's establisher.
Thee therefore, Oedipus, the mightiest head
Among us all, all we thy supplicants
Implore to find some way to succour us,
Whether thou knowest it through some voice from heaven,
Or, haply of some man; for I perceive
In men experienced that their counsels best
Find correspondence in things actual.
Haste thee, most absolute sir, be the state's builder!
Haste thee, look to it; doth not our country now
Call thee deliverer, for thy zeal of yore?
Never let us remember of thy rule

---

* Referring to Ismene, a legendary Theban woman.
** Athena.
*** The Sphinx, whose riddle Oedipus guessed.

That we stood once erectly, and then fell;
But build this city in stability!
With a fair augury didst thou shape for us
Our fortune then; like be thy prowess now!
If thou wilt rule this land (which thou art lord of),
It were a fairer lordship filled with folk
Than empty; towers and ships are nothingness,
Void of our fellow men to inhabit them.

OEDIPUS   Ah my poor children, what you come to seek
Is known already—not unknown to me.
You are all sick, I know it; and in your sickness
There is not one of you so sick as I.
For in your case his own particular pain
Comes to each singly; but my heart at once
Groans for the city, and for myself, and you.
Not therefore as one taking rest in sleep
Do you uprouse me; rather deem of me
As one that wept often, and often came
By many ways through labyrinths of care;
And the one remedy that I could find
By careful seeking—I supplied it. Creon,
Menoeceus' son, the brother of my queen,
I sent to Pytho, to Apollo's house,
To ask him by what act or word of mine
I might redeem this city; and the hours
Already measured even with today
Make me solicitous how he has sped;
For he is longer absent than the time
Sufficient, which is strange. When he shall come,
I were a wretch did I not then do all
As the God shews.

PRIEST   In happy time thou speak'st;
As these, who tell me Creon is at hand.

OEDIPUS   Ah King Apollo, might he but bring grace,
Radiant in fortune, as he is in face!

PRIEST   I think he comes with cheer; he would not, else,

Thus be approaching us with crown on brow,
All berries of the bay.

OEDIPUS   We shall know soon;
He is within hearing.

Enter CREON, *attended*.

                              My good lord and cousin,
Son of Menoeceus,
What answer of the God have you brought home?

CREON   Favourable; I mean, even what sounds ominously,
If it have issue in the way forthright,
May all end well.

OEDIPUS   How runs the oracle?
I am not confident, nor prone to fear
At what you say, so far.

CREON   If you desire
To hear while these stand near us, I am ready
To speak at once—or to go in with you.

OEDIPUS   Speak before all! My heavy load of care
More for their sake than for my own I bear.

CREON   What the God told me, that will I declare.
Phoebus our Lord gives us express command
To drive pollution, bred within this land,
Out of the country, and not cherish it
Beyond the power of healing.

OEDIPUS   By what purge?
What is the tenor of your tragedy?

CREON   Exile, or recompense of death for death;
Since 'tis this blood makes winter to the city.

OEDIPUS   Whose fate is this he signifies?

CREON   My liege,
We had a leader, once, over this land,
Called Laius—ere you held the helm of state.

OEDIPUS   So I did hear; I never saw the man.

CREON   The man is dead; and now, we are clearly bidden
To bring to account certain his murderers.

OEDIPUS   And where on earth are they? Where shall be found
          This dim-seen track-mark of an ancient crime?

CREON   "Within this land," it ran. That which is sought,
        That may be caught. What is unheeded scapes us.

OEDIPUS   Was it at home, afield, or anywhere
          Abroad, that Laius met this violent end?

CREON   He went professedly on pilgrimage;
        But since he started, came back home no more.

OEDIPUS   Nor any messenger nor way-fellow
          Looked on, from whom one might have learnt his story
          And used it?

CREON   No, they perished, all but one;
        He fled, affrighted; and of what he saw
        Had but one thing to say for certain.

OEDIPUS   Well,
          And what was that? one thing might be the means
          Of our discovering many, could we gain
          Some narrow ground for hope.

CREON   Robbers, he said,
        Met them, and slew him; by no single strength,
        But multitude of hands.

OEDIPUS   How could your robber
          Have dared so far—except there were some practice
          With gold from hence?

CREON   Why, it seemed probable.
        But, Laius dead, no man stood up to help
        Amid our ills.

OEDIPUS   What ill was in the way,
          Which, when a sovereignty had lapsed like this,
          Kept you from searching of it out?

CREON   The Sphinx
        With her enigma forced us to dismiss
        Things out of sight, and look to our own steps.

OEDIPUS   Well, I will have it all to light again.
          Right well did Phoebus, yea and well may you
          Insist on this observance toward the dead;

So shall you see me, as of right, with you,
Venging this country and the God together.
Why, 'tis not for my neighbours' sake, but mine,
I shall dispel this plague-spot; for the man,
Whoever it may be, who murdered him,
Lightly might hanker to serve me the same.
I benefit myself in aiding him.
Up then, my children, straightway, from the floor;
Take up your votive branches; let some other
Gather the tribes of Cadmus hitherward;
Say, I will make clean work. Please Heaven, our state
Shall soon appear happy, or desperate.

PRIEST   Come children, let us rise; it was for this,
Which he himself proclaims, that we came hither.
Now may the sender of these oracles,
In saving and in plague-staying, Phoebus, come!

> [*Exeunt* CREON, PRIEST *and* THEBANS.
> OEDIPUS *retires.*

Enter THEBAN SENATORS, *as Chorus.*

Chorus.

I. 1.

O Prophecy of Jove, whose words are sweet,
With what doom art thou sent
To glorious Thebes, from Pytho's gilded seat?
I am distraught with fearful wonderment,
I thrill with terror, and wait reverently—
Yea, Io Paean, Delian lord,* on thee!
What matter thou wilt compass—either strange,
Or once again recurrent as the seasons change,
Offspring of golden Hope, immortal Oracle,
Tell me, O tell!

* Apollo.

I. 2.

Athena first I greet with invocation,
Daughter of Jove, divine!
Next Artemis thy sister, of this nation
Keeper, high seated in the encircling shrine,
Filled with her praises, of our market-place,
And Phoebus, shooting arrows far through space;
Appear ye Three, the averters of my fate!
If e'er before, when mischief rose upon the state,
Ye quenched the flames of evil, putting them away,
Come—come to-day!

II. 1.

Woe, for unnumbered are the ills we bear!
Sickness pervades our hosts;
Nor is there any spear of guardian care,
Wherewith a man might save us, found in all our
        coasts.
For all the fair soil's produce now no longer springs;
Nor women from the labour and loud cries
Of their child-births arise;
And you may see, flying like a bird with wings,
One after one, outspeeding the resistless brand,
Pass—to the Evening Land.

II. 2.

In countless hosts our city perisheth.
Her children on the plain
Lie all unpitied—pitiless—breeding death.
Our wives meanwhile, and white-haired mothers in
        their train,
This way and that, suppliant, along the altar-side
Sit, and bemoan their doleful maladies;
Like flame their paeans rise,
With wailing and lament accompanied;

For whose dear sake O Goddess, O Jove's golden child,
Send Help with favour mild!

III. 1.

And Ares the Destroyer, him who thus—
Not now in harness of brass shields, as wont—
Ringed round with clamour, meets us front to front
And fevers us,
O banish from our country! Drive him back,
With winds upon his track,
On to the chamber vast of Amphitrite, *
Or that lone anchorage, the Thracian main;
For now, if night leave bounds to our annoy,
Day levels all again;
Wherefore, O father, Zeus, thou that dost wield the
might
Of fire-fraught light,
Him with thy bolt destroy!

III. 2.

Next, from the bendings of thy golden string
I would see showered thy artillery
Invincible, marshalled to succour me,
Lycean King!**
Next, those flame-bearing beams, arrows most bright,
Which Artemis by night
Through Lycian highlands speeds her scattering;
Thou too, the Evian, with thy Maenad band,
Thou golden-braided patron of this land
Whose visage glows with wine,
O save us from the god whom no gods honour! Hear,
Bacchus! Draw near,
And light thy torch of pine!

Enter OEDIPUS, *attended.*

* The sea.
** Apollo.

OEDIPUS   You are at prayers; but for your prayers' intent
You may gain help, and of your ills relief,
If you will minister to the pestilence,
And hearken and receive my words, which I—
A stranger to this tale, and to the deed
A stranger—shall pronounce; for of myself
I could not follow up the traces far,
Not having any key. But, made since then
A fellow-townsman to the townsmen here,
To all you Cadmeans I thus proclaim;
Whichever of you knows the man, by whom
Laius the son of Labdacus was slain,
Even if he is afraid, seeing he himself
Suppressed the facts that made against himself,
I bid that man shew the whole truth to me;
For he shall suffer no disparagement,
Except to quit the land, unscathed. Again,
If any knows another—say some stranger
To have been guilty, let him not keep silence;
For I will pay him the reward, and favour
Shall be his due beside it. But again,
If you will hold your peace, and any man
From self or friend in terror shall repel
This word of mine, then—you must hear me say
What I shall do. Whoe'er he be, I order
That of this land, whose power and throne are mine,
None entertain him, none accost him, none
Cause him to share in prayers or sacrifice
Offered to Heaven, or pour him lustral wave,
But all men from their houses banish him;
Since it is he contaminates us all,
Even as the Pythian oracle divine
Revealed but now to me. Such is my succour
Of him that's dead, and of the Deity.
And on the guilty head I imprecate
That whether by himself he has lain covert,
Or joined with others, without happiness,

Evil, in evil, he may pine and die.
And for myself I pray, if with my knowledge
He should become an inmate of my dwelling,
That I may suffer all that I invoked
On these just now. Moreover all these things
I charge you to accomplish, in behalf
Of me, and of the God, and of this land,
So ruined, barren and forsaken of Heaven.
For even though the matter were not now
By Heaven enjoined you, 'twas unnatural
For you to suffer it to pass uncleansed,
A man most noble having been slain, a king too!
Rather, you should have searched it out; but now,
Since I am vested with the government
Which he held once, and have his marriage-bed,
And the same wife; and since our progeny—
If his had not miscarried—had sprung from us
With common ties of common motherhood—
Only that Fate came heavy upon his head—
On these accounts I, as for my own father,
Will fight this fight, and follow out every clue,
Seeking to seize the author of his murder—
The scion of Labdacus and Polydore
And earlier Cadmus and Agenor old;
And such as disobey—the Gods I ask
Neither to raise them harvest from the ground
Nor children from the womb, but that they perish
By this fate present, and yet worse than this;
While you, the other Cadmeans, who approve,
May succouring Justice and all Gods in heaven
Accompany for good for evermore!

1 SENATOR   Even as thou didst adjure me, so, my king,
I will reply. I neither murdered him,
Nor can point out the murderer. For the quest—
To tell us who on earth has done this deed
Belonged to Phoebus, by whose word it came.

OEDIPUS   Your words are just; but to constrain the Gods
      To what they will not, passes all men's power.

1 SENATOR   I would say something which appears to me
      The second chance to this.

OEDIPUS   And your third, also—
      If such you have—by all means tell it.

1 SENATOR   Sir,
      Tiresias above all men, I am sure,
      Ranks as a seer next Phoebus, king with king;
      Of him we might enquire and learn the truth
      With all assurance.

OEDIPUS   That is what I did;
      And with no slackness; for by Creon's advice
      I sent, twice over; and for some time, now,
      'Tis strange he is not here.

1 SENATOR   Then all the rest
      Are but stale words and dumb.

OEDIPUS   What sort of words?
      I am weighing every utterance.

1 SENATOR   He was said
      To have been killed by footpads.

OEDIPUS   So I heard;
      But he who saw it is himself unseen.

1 SENATOR   Well, if his bosom holds a grain of fear,
      Curses like yours he never will abide!

OEDIPUS   Whom the doing awes not, speaking cannot scare.

1 SENATOR   Then there is one to expose him: here they come,
      Bringing the godlike seer, the only man
      Who has in him the tongue that cannot lie.

Enter TIRESIAS, *led by a boy.*

OEDIPUS   Tiresias, thou who searchest everything,
      Communicable or nameless, both in heaven
      And on the earth—thou canst not see the city,
      But knowest no less what pestilence visits it,
      Wherefrom our only saviour and defence

We find, sir king, in thee. For Phoebus—if
Thou dost not know it from the messengers—
To us, who sent to ask him, sent word back,
That from this sickness no release should come,
Till we had found and slain the men who slew
Laius, or driven them, banished, from the land.
Wherefore do thou—not sparing augury,
Either through birds, or any other way
Thou hast of divination—save thyself,
And save the city, and me; save the whole mass
By this dead corpse infected; for in thee
Stands our existence; and for men, to help
With might and main is of all tasks the highest.

TIRESIAS   Alas! How terrible it is to know,
Where no good comes of knowing! Of these matters
I was full well aware, but let them slip me;
Else I had not come hither.

OEDIPUS   But what is it?
How out of heart thou hast come!

TIRESIAS   Let me go home;
So shalt thou bear thy load most easily—
If thou wilt take my counsel—and I mine.

OEDIPUS   Thou hast not spoken loyally, nor friendly
Toward the State that bred thee, cheating her
Of this response!

TIRESIAS   Because I do not see
Thy words, not even thine, going to the mark;
So, not to be in the same plight—

1 SENATOR   For Heaven's sake,
If thou hast knowledge, do not turn away,
When all of us implore thee suppliant!

TIRESIAS   Ye
Are all unknowing; my say, in any sort,
I will not say, lest I display thy sorrow.

OEDIPUS   What, you do know, and will not speak? Your mind
Is to betray us, and destroy the city?

TIRESIAS   I will not bring remorse upon myself
And upon you. Why do you search these matters?
Vain, vain! I will not tell you.

OEDIPUS   Worst of traitors!
For you would rouse a very stone to wrath—
Will you not speak out ever, but stand thus
Relentless and persistent?

TIRESIAS   My offence
You censure; but your own, at home, you see not,
And yet blame me!

OEDIPUS   Who would not take offence,
Hearing the words in which you flout the city?

TIRESIAS   Well, it will come, keep silence as I may.

OEDIPUS   And what will come should I not hear from you?

TIRESIAS   I will declare no further. Storm at this,
If 't please you, to the wildest height of anger!

OEDIPUS   At least I will not, being so far in anger,
Spare anything of what is clear to me:
Know, I suspect you joined to hatch the deed;
Yea, did it—all but slaying with your own hands;
And if you were not blind, I should aver
The act was your work only!

TIRESIAS   Was it so?
I charge you to abide by your decree
As you proclaimed it; nor from this day forth
Speak word to these, or me; being of this land
Yourself the abominable contaminator!

OEDIPUS   So shamelessly set you this story on foot,
And think, perhaps, you shall go free?

TIRESIAS   I am
Free! for I have in me the strength of truth.

OEDIPUS   Who prompted you? for from your art it was not!

TIRESIAS   Yourself! You made me speak, against my will.

OEDIPUS   Speak! What? Repeat, that I may learn it better!

TIRESIAS   Did you not understand me at first hearing,
Or are you tempting me, when you say "Speak!"

OEDIPUS   Not so to say for certain; speak again.

TIRESIAS   I say that you are Laius' murderer—
    He whom you seek.

OEDIPUS   Not without chastisement
    Shall you, twice over, utter wounds!

TIRESIAS   Then shall I
    Say something more, that may incense you further?

OEDIPUS   Say what you please; it will be said in vain.

TIRESIAS   I say you know not in what worst of shame
    You live together with those nearest you,
    And see not in what evil plight you stand.

OEDIPUS   Do you expect to go on revelling
    In utterances like this?

TIRESIAS   Yes, if the truth
    Has any force at all.

OEDIPUS   Why so it has,
    Except for you; it is not so with you;
    Blind as you are in eyes, and ears, and mind!

TIRESIAS   Fool, you reproach me as not one of these
    Shall not reproach you, soon!

OEDIPUS   You cannot hurt me,
    Nor any other who beholds the light,
    Your life being all one night.

TIRESIAS   Nor is it fated
    You by my hand should fall; Apollo is
    Sufficient; he will bring it all to pass.

OEDIPUS   Are these inventions Creon's work, or yours?

TIRESIAS   Your bane is no-ways Creon, but your own self.

OEDIPUS   O riches, and dominion, and the craft
    That excels craft, and makes life enviable,
    How vast the grudge that is nursed up for you,
    When for this sovereignty, which the state
    Committed to my hands, unsought-for, free,
    Creon, the trusty, the familiar friend,
    With secret mines covets to oust me from it,
    And has suborned a sorcerer like this,

An engine-botching crafty cogging knave,
Who has no eyes to see with, but for gain,
And was born blind in the art! Why, tell me now,
How stand your claims to prescience? How came it,
When the oracular monster was alive,
You said no word to set this people free?
And yet it was not for the first that came
To solve her riddle; sooth was needed then,
Which you could not afford; neither from birds,
Nor any inspiration; till I came,
The unlettered Oedipus, and ended her,
By sleight of wit, untaught of augury—
I whom you now seek to cast out, in hope
To stand upon the steps of Creon's throne!
You and the framer of this plot methinks
Shall rue your purge for guilt! Dotard you seem,
Else by experience you had come to know
What thoughts these are you think!

1 SENATOR   As we conceive,
His words appear (and, Oedipus, your own,)
To have been said in anger; now not such
Our need, but rather to consider this—
How best to interpret the God's oracle.

TIRESIAS   King as you are, we must be peers at least
In argument; I am your equal, there;
For I am Loxias'* servant, and not yours;
So never need be writ of Creon's train.
And since you have reproached me with my blindness,
I say—you have your sight, and do not see
What evils are about you, nor with whom,
Nor in what home you are dwelling. Do you know
From whom you are? Yea, you are ignorant
That to your own you are an enemy,
Whether on earth, alive, or under it.

* Apollo's.

Soon from this land shall drive you, stalking grim,
Your mother's and your father's two-edged curse,
With eyes then dark, though they look proudly now.
What place on earth shall not be harbour, then,
For your lamenting? What Cithaeron-peak*
Shall not be resonant soon, when you discern
What hymen-song was that, which wafted you
On a fair voyage, to foul anchorage
Under yon roof? and multitudes besides
Of ills you know not of shall level you
Down to your self—down to your children! Go,
Trample on Creon, and on this mouth of mine;
But know, there is not one of all mankind
That shall be bruised more utterly than you.

OEDIPUS   Must I endure to hear all this from him?
Hence, to perdition! quickly hence! begone
Back from these walls, and turn you home again.

TIRESIAS   But that you called me, I had not come hither.

OEDIPUS   I did not know that you would utter folly;
Else I had scarce sent for you, to my house.

TIRESIAS   Yea, such is what we seem, foolish to you,
And to your fathers, who begat you, wise.

OEDIPUS   What fathers? Stop! Who was it gave me being?

TIRESIAS   This day shall give you birth and death in one.

OEDIPUS   How all too full of riddles and obscure
Is your discourse!

TIRESIAS   Were you not excellent
At solving riddles?

OEDIPUS   Ay, cast in my teeth
Matters in which you must allow my greatness!

TIRESIAS   And yet this very fortune was your ruin!

OEDIPUS   Well, if I saved this city, I care not.

TIRESIAS   Well,
I am going; and you, boy, take me home.

* Mountain associated with many myths; see also page 39.

OEDIPUS   Ay, let him.
>   Your turbulence impedes us, while you stay;
>   When you are gone, you can annoy no more.

[Retires.

TIRESIAS   I go, having said that I came to say;
>   Not that I fear your frown; for you possess
>   No power to kill me; but I say to you—
>   The man you have been seeking, threatening him,
>   And loud proclaiming him for Laius' murder,
>   That man is here; believed a foreigner
>   Here sojourning; but shall be recognized
>   For Theban born hereafter; yet not pleased
>   In the event; for blind instead of seeing,
>   And poor for wealthy, to a foreign land,
>   A staff to point his footsteps, he shall go.
>   Also to his own sons he shall be found
>   Related as a brother, though their sire,
>   And of the woman from whose womb he came
>   Both son and spouse; one that has raised up seed
>   To his own father, and has murdered him.
>   Now get you in, and ponder what I say;
>   And if you can detect me in a lie,
>   Then come and say that I am no true seer.

[Exeunt TIRESIAS *and Boy.*

Chorus.

I. 1.

>   Who is he, who was said
>   By the Delphian soothsaying rock
>   To have wrought with hands blood-red
>   Nameless unspeakable deeds?
>   Time it were that he fled
>   Faster than storm-swift steeds!
>   For upon him springs with a shock,
>   Armed in thunder and fire,

The Child of Jove, at the head.
　　Of the Destinies dread,
That follow, and will not tire.

I. 2.

For a word but now blazed clear
From Parnassus' snow-covered mound,*
To hunt down the Unknown!
He, through the forest drear,
By rocks, by cavernous ways,
Stalks, like a bull that strays,
Heartsore, footsore, alone;
Flying from Earth's central seat,
Flying the oracular sound
　　That with swift wings' beat
For ever circles him round.

II. 1.

Of a truth dark thoughts, yea dark and fell,
　　The augur wise doth arouse in me,
　　　　Who neither assent, nor yet gainsay;
And what to affirm, I cannot tell;
　　But I flutter in hope, unapt to see
　　　　Things of to-morrow, or to-day.

Why in Polybus' son** they should find a foe,
　　Or he in the heirs of Labdacus,
　　　　I know no cause, or of old, or late,
In test whereof I am now to go
　　Against the repute of Oedipus,
　　　　To avenge a Labdakid's unknown fate.

---

* Mount Parnassus is also associated with Apollo.
** Oedipus.

II. 2.

True, Zeus indeed, and Apollo, are wise,
  And knowers of what concerns mankind;
    But that word of a seer, a man like me,
Weighs more than mine, for a man to prize,
  Is all unsure. Yea, one man's mind
    May surpass another's in subtlety;

But never will I, till I see the rest,
  Assent to those who accuse him now.
    I saw how the air-borne Maiden came
Against him, and proved him wise, by the test,
  And good to the state; and for this, I trow,
    He shall not, ever, be put to shame.

Enter CREON.

CREON   I am come hither, fellow citizens,
  Having been told that Oedipus the king
  Lays grievous accusations to my charge,
  Which I will not endure. For if he fancies
  He in our present troubles has endured
  Aught at my hands, either in word or deed,
  Tending to harm him, I have no desire
  My life should be prolonged, bearing this blame.
  The injury that such a word may do
  Is no mere trifle, but more vast than any,
  If I am to be called a criminal
  Here in the town, and by my friends, and you.

1 SENATOR   Nay, the reproach, it may be, rather came
  Through stress of anger, than advisedly.

CREON   But it was plainly said, by my advice
  The prophet gave false answers.

1 SENATOR   It was said;
  But how advised I know not.

CREON   Was this charge

           Of a set mind, and with set countenance
           Imputed against me?

1 SENATOR   I do not know.
           I have no eyes for what my masters do.
           But here he comes, himself, forth of the palace.

Enter OEDIPUS.

OEDIPUS   Fellow, how cam'st thou hither? Dost thou boast
           So great a front of daring, as to come
           Under my roof, the assassin clear of me,
           And manifest pirate of my royalty?
           Tell me, by heaven, did you detect in me
           The bearing of a craven, or a fool,
           That you laid plans to do it; or suppose
           I should not recognize your work in this,
           Creeping on slily, and defend myself?
           Is it not folly, this attempt of yours,
           Without a following, without friends, to hunt
           After a throne, a thing which is achieved
           By aid of followers and much revenue?

CREON   Do me this favour; hear me say as much
           As you have said; and then, yourself decide.

OEDIPUS   You are quick to talk, but I am slow to learn
           Of you; for I have found you contrary
           And dangerous to me.

CREON   Now, this same thing
           First hear, how I shall state it.

OEDIPUS   This same thing
           Do not tell me—that you are not a villain!

CREON   If you suppose your arrogance weighs aught
           Apart from reason, you are much astray.

OEDIPUS   If you suppose you can escape the pain
           Due for a kinsman's wrong, you are astray!

CREON   You speak with justice; I agree! But tell me,
           How is it that you say I injured you?

OEDIPUS   Did you persuade me that I ought to send
           To fetch that canting soothsayer, or no?

CREON Why yes, and now, I am of the same mind, still.

OEDIPUS How long is it since Laius—

CREON What? I know not.

OEDIPUS Died—disappeared, murdered by violence?

CREON Long seasons might be numbered, long gone by.

OEDIPUS Well, did this seer then practise in the craft?

CREON Yes, just as wise, and just as much revered.

OEDIPUS And did he at that time say one word of me?

CREON Well, nowhere in my presence, anyhow.

OEDIPUS But did not you hold inquest for the dead?

CREON We did, of course; and got no evidence.

OEDIPUS Well then, how came it that this wiseacre
Did not say these things then?

CREON I do not know.
In matters where I have no cognizance
I hold my tongue.

OEDIPUS This much, at least, you know,
And if you are wise, will say!

CREON And what is that?
For if I know it, I shall not refuse.

OEDIPUS Why, that unless he had conspired with you
He never would have said that Laius' murder
Was of my doing!

CREON If he says so, you know.
Only I claim to know that first from you,
Which you put now to me.

OEDIPUS Learn anything!
For I shall not be found a murderer.

CREON Well then; you have my sister to your wife?

OEDIPUS There's no denying that question.

CREON And with her
Rule equal, and in common hold the land?

OEDIPUS All she may wish for she obtains of me.

CREON And make I not a third, equal with you?

OEDIPUS Ay, there appears your friendship's falsity.

CREON Not if you reason with yourself, as I.
And note this first; if you can think that any

Would rather choose a sovereignty, with fears,
Than the same power, with undisturbed repose?
Neither am I, by nature, covetous
To be a king, rather than play the king,
Nor any man who has sagacity.
Now I have all things, without fear, from you;
Reigned I myself, I must do much I hated.
How were a throne, then, pleasanter for me
Than painless empire and authority?
I am not yet so blinded as to wish
For honour, other than is joined with gain.
Now am I hail-fellow-well-met with all;
Now every man gives me good-morrow; now
The waiters on your favour fawn on me;
For all their prospering depends thereby.
Then how should I exchange this lot for yours?
A mind well balanced cannot turn to crime.
I neither am in love with this design,
Nor, in a comrade, would I suffer it.
For proof of which, first, go to Pytho; ask
For the oracles, if I declared them truly;
Next, if you can detect me in the act
Of any conjuration with the seer,
Then, by a double vote, not one alone,
Mine and your own, take me, and take my life;
But do not, on a dubious argument,
Charge me beside the facts. For just it is not,
To hold bad men for good, good men for bad,
To no good end; nay, 'twere all one to me
To throw away a friend, a worthy one,
And one's own life, which most of all one values.
Ah well; in time, you will see these things plainly;
For time alone shews a man's honesty,
But in one day you may discern his guilt.

1 SENATOR   His words sound fair—to one who fears to fall;
            For swift in counsel is unsafe, my liege.

OEDIPUS   When he who plots against me in the dark

Comes swiftly on, I must be swift in turn.
If I stay quiet, his ends will have been gained,
And mine all missed.

CREON   What is it that you want?
To expel me from the country?

OEDIPUS   Not at all.
Your death I purpose, not your banishment.

CREON   Not without shewing, first, what a thing is jealousy!

OEDIPUS   You talk like one who will not yield, nor heed.

CREON   Because I see you mean injuriously.

OEDIPUS   Not to myself!

CREON   No more you ought to me!

OEDIPUS   You are a traitor!

CREON   What if you are no judge?

OEDIPUS   I must be ruler.

CREON   Not if you rule badly.

OEDIPUS   City, my city!

CREON   The city is mine too,
And not yours only.

1 SENATOR   Good my lords, have done,
Here is Jocasta; in good time, I see her
Come to you from the palace; with her aid
'Twere meet to appease your present difference.

Enter JOCASTA.

JOCASTA   Unhappy men, what was it made you raise
This senseless broil of words? Are you not both
Ashamed of stirring private grievances,
The land being thus afflicted? Get you in—
And, Creon, do you go home; push not mere nothing
On to some terrible calamity!

CREON   Sister, your husband Oedipus thinks fit
To treat me villainously; choosing for me
Of two bad things, one; to expatriate me,
Or seize and kill me.

OEDIPUS   I admit it, wife;

For I have found him out in an offence
Against my person, joined with treachery.

CREON   So may I never thrive, but perish, banned
Of Heaven, if I have done a thing to you
Of what you charge against me!

JOCASTA   Oedipus!
O in Heaven's name believe it! Above all
Revere this oath in heaven; secondly
Myself, and these, who stand before you here.

1 SENATOR   Hear her, my king! With wisdom and goodwill
I pray you hear!

OEDIPUS   What would you have me grant?

1 SENATOR   Respect his word; no bauble, heretofore;
And by this oath made weighty.

OEDIPUS   Do you know
For what you ask?

1 SENATOR   I do.

OEDIPUS   Say what you mean, then!

1 SENATOR   That you expel not, ever, with disgrace,
The friend, who has abjured it, on a charge
Void of clear proof.

OEDIPUS   Now, understand it well;
Seek this, you seek my death or exile!

1 SENATOR   Nay,
By the Sun-god, first of all Gods in heaven!
So may I perish, to the uttermost,
Cut off from Heaven, without the help of men,
If I have such a thought! But the land's waste
Will break my heart with grief—and that this woe,
Your strife, is added to its former woe.

OEDIPUS   Well, let him go, though I get slain outright,
Or thrust by force, dishonoured, from the land;
Your voice, not his, makes me compassionate,
Pleading for pity; he, where'er he be,
Shall have my hatred.

CREON   You display your spleen

In yielding; but, when your wrath passes bound,
Are formidable! Tempers such as yours
Most grievous are to their own selves to bear,
Not without justice.

OEDIPUS   Leave me; get you gone!

CREON   I go; you know me not; these know me honest.

[*Exit.*

1 SENATOR   Lady, what hinders you from taking him
    Into the house?

JOCASTA   I would know how this happened.

1 SENATOR   A blind surmise arose, out of mere babble;
    But even what is unjust inflicts a sting.

JOCASTA   On part of both?

1 SENATOR   Yes truly.

JOCASTA   And what was said?

1 SENATOR   Enough it seems, enough it seems to me,
    Under the former trouble of the land,
    To leave this where it lies.

OEDIPUS   Do you perceive
    How far you are carried—a well-meaning man!
    Slurring my anger thus, and blunting it?

1 SENATOR   I said it, O my king, not once alone—
    But be assured, I should have shewn myself
    Robbed of my wits, useless for work of wit,
    Renouncing thee! who didst impel the sails
    Of my dear land, baffled mid straits, right onward,
    And it may be, wilt waft her safely now!

JOCASTA   For Heaven's sake tell me too, my lord, what was it
    Caused you so deep an anger?

OEDIPUS   I will tell you;
    For I respect you, lady, more than these;
    'Twas Creon—at plots which he has laid for me.

JOCASTA   If you will charge the quarrel in plain terms,
    Why speak!

OEDIPUS   He says that I am Laius' slayer.

JOCASTA   Of his own knowledge, or on hearsay?

OEDIPUS   Nay,
    But by citation of a knavish seer;
    As for himself, he keeps his words blame-free.

JOCASTA   Now set you free from thought of that you talk of;
    Listen and learn, nothing in human life
    Turns on the soothsayer's art. Tokens of this
    I'll show you in few words. To Laius once
    There came an oracle, I do not say
    From Phoebus' self, but from his ministers,
    That so it should befall, that he should die
    By a son's hands, whom he should have by me.
    And him—the story goes—robbers abroad
    Have murdered, at a place where three roads meet;
    While from our son's birth not three days went by
    Before, with ankles pinned, he cast him out,
    By hands of others, on a pathless moor.
    And so Apollo did not bring about
    That he should be his father's murderer;
    Nor yet that Laius should endure the stroke
    At his son's hands, of which he was afraid.
    This is what came of soothsayers' oracles;
    Whereof take thou no heed. That which we lack,
    If a God seek, himself will soon reveal.

OEDIPUS   What perturbation and perplexity
    Take hold upon me, woman, hearing you!

JOCASTA   What stress of trouble is on you, that you say so?

OEDIPUS   I thought I heard you say Laius was slain
    Where three roads meet!

JOCASTA   Yes, so the rumour ran,
    And so runs still.

OEDIPUS   And where might be the spot
    Where this befell?

JOCASTA   Phocis the land is named;
    There are two separate roads converge in one
    From Daulia and Delphi.

OEDIPUS   And what time
    Has passed since then?

JOCASTA   It was but just before
      You were installed as ruler of the land,
      The tidings reached the city.
OEDIPUS   God of Heaven!
      What would'st thou do unto me!
JOCASTA   Oedipus,
      What is it on your mind?
OEDIPUS   Ask me not yet.
      But Laius—say, what was he like? what prime
      Of youth had he attained to?
JOCASTA   He was tall;
      The first white flowers had blossomed in his hair;
      His figure was not much unlike your own.
OEDIPUS   Me miserable! It seems I have but now
      Proffered myself to a tremendous curse
      Not knowing!
JOCASTA   How say you? I tremble, O my lord,
      To gaze upon you!
OEDIPUS   I am sore afraid
      The prophet was not blind; but you will make
      More certain, if you answer one thing more.
JOCASTA   Indeed I tremble; but the thing you ask
      I'll answer, when I know it.
OEDIPUS   Was he going
      Poorly attended, or with many spears
      About him, like a prince?
JOCASTA   But five in all;
      One was a herald; and one carriage held
      Laius himself,
OEDIPUS   O, it is plain already!
      Woman, who was it told this tale to you?
JOCASTA   A servant, who alone came safe away.
OEDIPUS   Is he perchance now present, in the house?
JOCASTA   Why no; for after he was come from thence,
      And saw you governing, and Laius dead,
      He came and touched my hand, and begged of me
      To send him to the fields and sheep-meadows,

       So he might be as far as possible
       From eyesight of the townsmen; and I sent him;
       For he was worthy, for a slave, to obtain
       Even greater favours.

OEDIPUS   Could we have him back
       Quickly?

JOCASTA   We could. But why this order?

OEDIPUS   Wife,
       I fear me I have spoken far too much;
       Wherefore I wish to see him.

JOCASTA   He shall come!
       But I am worthy, in my turn, to know
       What weighs so heavily upon you, Sir?

OEDIPUS   And you shall know; since I have passed so far
       The bounds of apprehension. For to whom
       Could I impart, passing through such a need,
       Greater in place—if that were all—than you?
       —I am the son of Polybus of Corinth,
       And of a Dorian mother, Merope.
       And I was counted most preëminent
       Among the townsmen there; up to the time
       A circumstance befell me, of this fashion—
       Worthy of wonder, though of my concern
       Unworthy. At the board a drunken fellow
       Over his cups called me a changeling;
       And I, being indignant—all that day
       Hardly refrained—but on the morrow went
       And taxed my parents with it to their face;
       Who took the scandal grievously, of him
       Who launched the story. Well, with what they said
       I was content; and yet the thing still galled me;
       For it spread far. So without cognizance
       Of sire or mother I set out to go
       To Pytho.* Phoebus sent me of my quest

---

* The Pythian oracle at Delphi, as on page 5.

Bootless away; but other terrible
And strange and lamentable things revealed,
Saying I should wed my mother, and produce
A race intolerable for men to see,
And be my natural father's murderer.
When I heard that, measuring where Corinth stands
Even thereafter by the stars alone,
Where I might never think to see fulfilled
The scandals of ill prophecies of me,
I fled, an exile. As I journeyed on,
I found myself upon the self-same spot
Where, you say, this king perished. In your ears,
Wife, I will tell the whole. When in my travels
I was come near this place where three roads meet,
There met me a herald, and a man that rode
In a colt-carriage, as you tell of him,
And from the track the leader, by main force,
And the old man himself, would thrust me. I,
Being enraged, strike him who jostled me—
The driver—and the old man, when he saw it,
Watching as I was passing, from the car
With his goad's fork smote me upon the head.
He paid, though! duly I say not; but in brief,
Smitten by the staff in this right hand of mine,
Out of the middle of the carriage straight
He rolls down headlong; and I slay them all!
But if there be a semblance to connect
This nameless man with Laius, who is now
More miserable than I am? Who on earth
Could have been born with more of hate from heaven?
Whom never citizen or stranger may
Receive into their dwellings, or accost,
But must thrust out of doors; and 'tis no other
Laid all these curses on myself, than I!
Yea, with embraces of the arms whereby
He perished, I pollute my victim's bed!

Am I not vile? Am I not all unclean?
If I must fly, and flying, never can
See my own folk, or on my native land
Set foot, or else must with my mother wed,
And slay my father Polybus, who begat
And bred me? Would he not speak truly of me
Who judged these things sent by some barbarous Power?
Never, you sacred majesties of Heaven,
Never may I behold that day; but pass
Out of men's sight, ere I shall see myself
Touched by the stain of such a destiny!

1 SENATOR   My liege, these things affect us grievously;
    Still, till you hear his story who was by,
    Do not lose hope!

OEDIPUS   Yea, so much hope is left,
    Merely to wait for him, the herdsman.

JOCASTA   Well,
    Suppose him here, what do you want of him?

OEDIPUS   I'll tell you; if he should be found to say
    Just what you said, I shall be clear from harm.

JOCASTA   What did you hear me say, that did not tally?

OEDIPUS   You were just telling me that he made mention
    Of "robbers"—"men"—as Laius' murderers.
    Now if he shall affirm their number still,
    I did not slay him. One cannot be the same
    As many. But if he shall speak of one—
    One only, it is evident this deed
    Already will have been brought home to me.

JOCASTA   But be assured, that was the word, quite plainly!
    And now he cannot blot it out again.
    Not I alone, but the whole city heard it.
    Then, even if he shift from his first tale,
    Not so, my lord, will he at all explain
    The death of Laius, as it should have been,
    Whom Loxias declared my son must slay!
    And after all, the poor thing never killed him,

But died itself before! so that henceforth
I do not mean to look to left or right
For fear of soothsaying!

OEDIPUS   You are well advised.
Still, send and fetch the labourer; do not miss it.

JOCASTA   I will send quickly. Now let us go within.
I would do nothing that displeases you.

> [*Exeunt* OEDIPUS *and* JOCASTA.

Chorus.

I. 1.

Let it be mine to keep
The holy purity of word and deed
Foreguided all by mandates from on high
Born in the ethereal region of the sky,
Their only sire Olympus; them nor seed
Of mortal man brought forth, nor Lethe cold
Shall ever lay to sleep;
In them Deity is great, and grows not old.

I. 2.

Pride is the germ of kings;
Pride, when puffed up, vainly, with many things
Unseasonable, unfitting, mounts the wall,
Only to hurry to that fatal fall,
Where feet are vain to serve her. But the task
Propitious to the city GOD I ask
Never to take away!
GOD I will never cease to hold my stay.

II. 1.

But if any man proceed
Insolently in word or deed,
Without fear of right, or care

For the seats where Virtues are,
Him, for his ill-omened pride,
Let an evil death betide!
If honestly his gear he will not gain,
    Nor keep himself from deeds unholy,
Nor from inviolable things abstain,
        Blinded by folly.
In such a course, what mortal from his heart
        Dart upon dart
Can hope to avert of indignation?
Yea, and if acts like these are held in estimation,
        Why dance we here our part?

II. 2.

Never to the inviolate hearth
At the navel of the earth,*
Nor to Abae's fane, in prayer,
Nor the Olympian, will I fare,
If it shall not so befall
Manifestly unto all.
But O our king—if thou art named aright—
    Zeus, that art Lord of all things ever,
Be this not hid from Thee, nor from Thy might
        Which endeth never.
For now already men invalidate
        The dooms of Fate
Uttered for Laius, fading slowly;
Apollo's name and rites are nowhere now kept holy;
        Worship is out of date.

Enter JOCASTA, *attended.*

JOCASTA   Lords of the land, it came into my heart
        To approach the temples of the Deities,
        Taking in hand these garlands, and this incense;

---

* The oracle at Delphi.

For Oedipus lets his mind float too light
Upon the eddies of all kinds of grief;
Nor will he, like a man of soberness,
Measure the new by knowledge of the old,
But is at mercy of whoever speaks,
If he but speak the language of despair.
I can do nothing by exhorting him.
Wherefore, Lycean Phoebus, unto thee—
For thou art very near us—I am come.
Bringing these offerings, a petitioner
That thou afford us fair deliverance;
Since now we are all frighted, seeing him—
The vessel's pilot, as 'twere—panic-stricken.

Enter a Messenger.

MESSENGER   Sirs, might I learn of you, where is the palace
        Of Oedipus the King? or rather, where
        He is himself, if you know, tell me.
1 SENATOR   Stranger,
        This is his dwelling, and he is within;
        This lady is his children's mother, too.
MESSENGER   A blessing ever be on hers and her,
        Who is, in such a perfect sort, his wife!
JOCASTA   The like be with you too, as you deserve,
        Sir, for your compliment. But say what end
        You come for, and what news you wish to tell.
MESSENGER   Good to the house, and to your husband, lady.
JOCASTA   Of what sort? and from whom come you?
MESSENGER   From Corinth.
        In that which I am now about to say
        May you find pleasure! and why not? And yet
        Perhaps you may be sorry.
JOCASTA   But what is it?
        How can it carry such ambiguous force?
MESSENGER   The dwellers in the land of Isthmia,
        As was there said, intend to appoint him king.

JOCASTA   What! Is not Polybus, the old prince, still reigning?

MESSENGER   No, truly; he is Death's subject, in the grave.

JOCASTA   How say you, father? Is Polybus no more?

MESSENGER   I stake my life upon it, if I lie!

JOCASTA   Run, girl, and tell your master instantly.

[*Exit an attendant.*

> O prophecies of Gods, where are you now!
> Oedipus fled, long since, from this man's presence,
> Fearing to kill him; and now he has died
> A natural death, not by his means at all!

Enter OEDIPUS.

OEDIPUS   O my most dear Jocasta, wife of mine,
Why did you fetch me hither from the house?

JOCASTA   Hear this man speak! Listen and mark, to what
The dark responses of the God are come!

OEDIPUS   And who is this? What says he?

JOCASTA   He's from Corinth,
To tell us that your father Polybus
Lives no more, but is dead!

OEDIPUS   What say you, sir?
Tell your own tale yourself.

MESSENGER   If first of all
I must deliver this for certainty,
Know well, that he has gone the way of mortals.

OEDIPUS   Was it by treason, or some chance disease?

MESSENGER   A little shock prostrates an aged frame!

OEDIPUS   Sickness, you mean, was my poor father's end?

MESSENGER   Yes, and old age; his term of life was full.

OEDIPUS   Heigh ho! Why, wife! why should a man regard
The oracular hearth of Pytho, or the birds
Cawing above us, by whose canons I
Was to have slain my father? He is dead,
And buried out of sight; and here am I,
Laying no finger to the instrument,
(Unless, indeed, he pined for want of me,

And so, I killed him!) Well, Polybus is gone;
And with him all those oracles of ours
Bundled to Hades, for old songs, together!

JOCASTA   Did I not say so all along?

OEDIPUS   You did;
But I was led astray by fear.

JOCASTA   Well, now
Let none of these predictions any more
Weigh on your mind!

OEDIPUS   And how can I help dreading
My mother's bed?

JOCASTA   But why should men be fearful,
O'er whom Fortune is mistress, and foreknowledge
Of nothing sure? Best take life easily,
As a man may. For that maternal wedding,
Have you no fear; for many men ere now
Have dreamed as much; but he who by such dreams
Sets nothing, has the easiest life of it.

OEDIPUS   All these things would have been well said of you,
Were not my mother living still; but now,
She being alive, there is all need of dread;
Though you say well.

JOCASTA   And yet your father's burial
Lets in much daylight!

OEDIPUS   I acknowledge, much.
Still, her who lives I fear.

MESSENGER   But at what woman
Are you dismayed?

OEDIPUS   At Merope, old man,
The wife of Polybus.

MESSENGER   And what of her
Causes you terror?

OEDIPUS   A dark oracle,
Stranger, from heaven.

MESSENGER   May it be put in words?
Or is it wrong another man should know it?

OEDIPUS   No, not at all. Why, Loxias declared
            That I should one day marry my own mother,
            And with my own hands shed my father's blood.
            Wherefore from Corinth I have kept away
            Far, for long years; and prospered; none the less
            It is most sweet to see one's parents' face.

MESSENGER   And in this apprehension you became
            An emigrant from Corinth?

OEDIPUS   And, old man,
            Desiring not to be a parricide.

MESSENGER   Why should I not deliver you, my liege—
            Since my intent in coming here was good—
            Out of this fear?

OEDIPUS   Indeed you would obtain
            Good guerdon from me.

MESSENGER   And indeed for this
            Chiefest I came, that upon your return
            I might in some sort benefit.

OEDIPUS   But I
            Will never go, to meet my parents there!

MESSENGER   O son, 'tis plain you know not what you do!

OEDIPUS   How so, old man? in Heaven's name tell me!

MESSENGER   If
            On this account you shun the journey home!

OEDIPUS   Of course I fear lest Phoebus turn out true.

MESSENGER   Lest through your parents you incur foul stain?

OEDIPUS   Yes, father, yes; that is what always scares me.

MESSENGER   Now do you know you tremble, really, at nothing?

OEDIPUS   How can that be, if I was born their child?

MESSENGER   Because Polybus was nought akin to you!

OEDIPUS   What, did not Polybus beget me?

MESSENGER   No,
            No more than I did; just so much as I!

OEDIPUS   How, my own sire no more than—nobody?

MESSENGER   But neither he begat you, nor did I.

OEDIPUS   Then from what motive did he call me son?

MESSENGER   Look here; he had you as a gift from me.

OEDIPUS   And loved me then, so much, at second hand?

MESSENGER   Yes, his long childlessness prevailed on him.

OEDIPUS   And did you find or purchase me, to give him?

MESSENGER   I found you in Cithaeron's wooded dells.

OEDIPUS   How came you to be journeying in these parts?

MESSENGER   I tended flocks upon the mountains here.

OEDIPUS   You were a shepherd, and you ranged for hire?

MESSENGER   But at the same time your preserver, son!

OEDIPUS   You found me in distress? What was my trouble?

MESSENGER   Your ankle joints may witness.

OEDIPUS   O, why speak you
        Of that old evil?

MESSENGER   I untied you, when
        You had the soles of both your feet bored through.

OEDIPUS   A shameful sort of swaddling bands were mine.

MESSENGER   Such, that from them you had the name you bear.*

OEDIPUS   Tell me, by heaven! at sire's or mother's hand—

MESSENGER   I know not: he who gave you knows of that
        Better than I.

OEDIPUS   You got me from another?
        You did not find me?

MESSENGER   No, another shepherd
        Gave you to me.

OEDIPUS   Who was he? are you able
        To point him out?

MESSENGER   They said that he was one
        Of those who followed Laius, whom you know.

OEDIPUS   Him who was once the monarch of this land?

MESSENGER   Precisely! This man was his herdsman.

OEDIPUS   Now
        Is this man still alive for me to see?

MESSENGER   You must know best, the people of the place.

OEDIPUS   Is any here among you bystanders,

* By a folk etymology, the name Oedipus is taken to mean "swollen feet."

Who knows the herdsman whom he tells us of,
From seeing him, either in the fields or here?
Speak! it were time that this had been cleared up.

1 SENATOR   I think he is no other than that peasant
Whom you were taking pains to find, before;
But she could say as well as any one—
Jocasta.

OEDIPUS   Lady, you remember him
Whose coming we were wishing for but now;
Does he mean him?

JOCASTA   Why ask who 'twas he spoke of?
Nay, never mind—never remember it—
'Twas idly spoken!

OEDIPUS   Nay, it cannot be
That having such a clue I should refuse
To solve the mystery of my parentage!

JOCASTA   For Heaven's sake, if you care for your own life,
Don't seek it! I am sick, and that's enough!

OEDIPUS   Courage! At least, if I be thrice a slave,
Born so three-deep, it cannot injure you!

JOCASTA   But I beseech you, hearken! Do not do it!

OEDIPUS   I will not hearken—not to know the whole.

JOCASTA   I mean well; and I tell you for the best!

OEDIPUS   What you call best is an old sore of mine.

JOCASTA   Wretch, what thou art O might'st thou never know!

OEDIPUS   Will some one go and fetch the herdsman hither?
She is welcome to her gilded lineage!

JOCASTA   O
Woe, woe, unhappy! This is all I have
To say to thee, and no word more, for ever!

                                                        [*Exit.*

1 SENATOR   Why has the woman vanished, Oedipus,
Driven so wild with grief? I am afraid
Out of her silence will break forth some trouble.

OEDIPUS   Break out what will, I shall not hesitate,
Low though it be, to trace the source of me.

But she, perhaps, being, as a woman, proud,
Of my unfit extraction is ashamed.
—I deem myself the child of Fortune! I
Shall not be shamed of her, who favours me;
Seeing I have her for mother; and for kin
The limitary Moons, that found me small,
That fashioned me for great! Parented thus,
How could I ever in the issue prove
Other—that I should leave my birth unknown?

Chorus

1.

If I am a true seer,
    My mind from error clear,
Tomorrow's moon shall not pass over us,
    Ere, O Cithaeron, we
    Shall magnify in thee
The land, the lap, the womb of Oedipus;
And we shall hymn thy praises, for good things
Of thy bestowing, done unto our kings.
Yea, Phoebus, if thou wilt, amen, so might it be!

2.

Who bare thee? Which, O child,
    Over the mountain-wild
Sought to by Pan of the immortal Maids?
    Or Loxias—was he
    The sire who fathered thee?
For dear to him are all the upland glades.
Was it Cyllene's lord* acquired a son,
    Or Bacchus, dweller on the heights, from one
Of those he liefest loves, Oreads** of Helicon?

* Hermes.
** Mountain nymphs.

Enter Attendants with an Old Man, a Shepherd.

OEDIPUS   If I may guess, who never met with him,
   I think I see that herdsman, Senators,
   We have long been seeking; for his ripe old age
   Harmoniously accords with this man's measure;
   Besides, I recognize the men who bring him
   As of my household; but in certainty
   You can perhaps exceed me, who beheld
   The herdsman formerly.

1 SENATOR   Why, to be sure,
   I recognize him; for he was a man
   Trusty as any Laius ever had
   About his pastures.

OEDIPUS   You I ask the first,
   The Corinthian stranger; do you speak of him?

MESSENGER   Yes, him you see.

OEDIPUS   Sirrah, old man, look here;
   Answer my questions. Were you Laius' man?

OLD MAN   Truly his thrall; not bought, but bred at home.

OEDIPUS   Minding what work, or in what character?

OLD MAN   Most of my time I went after the flocks.

OEDIPUS   In what directions, chiefly, were your folds?

OLD MAN   There was Cithaeron; and a bit near by.

OEDIPUS   Do you know this man, then? Did you see him there?

OLD MAN   Him? After what? What man do you mean?

OEDIPUS   This fellow
   Here present; did you ever meet with him?

OLD MAN   Not so to say off-hand, from memory.

MESSENGER   And that's no wonder, sir; but beyond doubt
   I will remind him, though he has forgotten,
   I am quite sure he knows, once on a time,
   When in the bit about Cithaeron there—
   He with two flocks together, I with one—
   I was his neighbour for three whole half years
   From spring-tide onward to the Bear-ward's* day;

---

* The constellation Bootes.

And with the winter to my folds I drove,
And he to Laius' stables. Are these facts,
Or are they not—what I am saying?

OLD MAN   Yes,
You speak the truth; but it was long ago.

MESSENGER   Come, say now, don't you mind that you then gave me
A baby boy to bring up for my own?

OLD MAN   What do you mean? Why do you ask it me?

MESSENGER   This is the man, good fellow; who was then
A youngling!

OLD MAN   Out upon you! Hold your peace!

OEDIPUS   Nay, old man, do not chide him; for your words
Deserve a chiding rather than his own!

OLD MAN   O best of masters, what is my offence?

OEDIPUS   Not telling of that boy he asks about.

OLD MAN   He says he knows not what! He is all astray!

OEDIPUS   You will not speak of grace—you shall perforce!

OLD MAN   Do not for God's sake harm me, an old man!

OEDIPUS   Quick, some one, twist his hands behind him!

OLD MAN   Wretch,
What have I done? What do you want to know?

OEDIPUS   Did you give him that boy he asks about?

OLD MAN   I gave it him. Would I had died that day!

OEDIPUS   Tell the whole truth, or you will come to it!

OLD MAN   I am undone far more, though, if I speak!

OEDIPUS   The man is trifling with us, I believe.

OLD MAN   No, no; I said I gave it, long ago!

OEDIPUS   Where did you get it? At home, or from some other?

OLD MAN   It was not mine; another gave it me.

OEDIPUS   Which of these citizens? and from what roof?

OLD MAN   Don't, master, for God's sake, don't ask me more!

OEDIPUS   You are a dead man, if I speak again!

OLD MAN   Then—'twas a child—of Laius' household.

OEDIPUS   What,
Slave-born? or one of his own family?

OLD MAN   O, I am at the horror, now, to speak!

OEDIPUS   And I to hear. But I must hear—no less.

OLD MAN   Truly it was called his son; but she within,
       Your lady, could best tell you how it was.
OEDIPUS   Did she then give it you?
OLD MAN   My lord, even so.
OEDIPUS   For what?
OLD MAN   For me to make away with it.
OEDIPUS   Herself the mother? miserable!
OLD MAN   In dread
       Of evil prophecies—
OEDIPUS   What prophecies?
OLD MAN   That he should kill his parents, it was said.
OEDIPUS   How came you then to give it to this old man?
OLD MAN   For pity, O my master! thinking he
       Would carry it away to other soil,
       From whence he came; but he to the worst of harms
       Saved it! for if thou art the man he says,
       Sure thou wast born destined to misery!
OEDIPUS   Woe! woe! It is all plain, indeed! O Light,
       This be the last time I shall gaze on thee,
       Who am revealed to have been born of those
       Of whom I ought not—to have wedded whom
       I ought not—and slain whom I might not slay!

                       [*Exit.*

Chorus.

I. 1.

    O generations of mankind!
        How do I find
         Your lives nought worth at all!
    For who is he—what state
    Is there, more fortunate
    Than only to seem great,
        And then, to fall?
    I having thee for pattern, and thy lot—
    Thine, O poor Oedipus—I envy not

Aught in mortality;
For this is he

I. 2.

Who, shooting far beyond the rest,
Won wealth all-blest,
Slaying, Zeus, thy monster-maid,
Crook-taloned, boding; and
Who did arise and stand
Betwixt death and our land,
A tower of aid;
Yea for this cause thou hast been named our king,
And honoured in the highest, governing
The city of Thebae great
In royal state.

II. 1.

And now, who lives more utterly undone?
Who with sad woes, who with mischances rude
Stands closer yokèd by life's vicissitude?
O honoured head of Oedipus, for whom
Within the same wide haven there was room
To come—child, to the birth—
Sire, to the nuptial bower,
How could the furrows of thy parent earth—
How could they suffer thee, O hapless one,
In silence, to this hour?

II. 2.

Time found thee out—Time who sees everything—
Unwittingly guilty; and arraigns thee now
Consort ill-sorted, unto whom are bred
Sons of thy getting, in thine own birth-bed.
O scion of Laius' race,

> Would I had never never seen thy face!
> For I lament, even as from lips that sing
> Pouring a dirge; yet verily it was thou
> Gav'st me to rise
> And breathe again, and close my watching eyes.

Enter a second MESSENGER.

2 MESSENGER   O you most honoured ever of this land,
What deeds have you to hear, what sights to see,
What sorrow to endure, if you still cherish
The house of Labdacus with loyalty?
For Ister* I suppose or Phasis'** wave
Never could purge this dwelling from the ills
It covers—or shall instantly reveal,
Invited, not inflicted; of all wounds,
Those that seem wilful are the worst to bear.

1 SENATOR   There was no lack, in what we knew before,
Of lamentable; what have you more to say?

2 MESSENGER   The speediest of all tales to hear and tell;
The illustrious Jocasta is no more.

1 SENATOR   Unhappy woman! From what cause?

2 MESSENGER   Self-slain.
Of what befell the saddest part is spared;
For you were not a witness. None the less
So far as I can tell it you shall hear
Her miserable story. When she passed
So frantically inside the vestibule,
She went straight onward to the bed-chamber,
With both her hands tearing her hair; the doors
She dashed to as she entered, crying out
On Laius, long since dead, calling to mind
His fore-begotten offspring, by whose hands
He, she said, died, and left to his own seed

* The Danube.
** A river emptying into the Black Sea.

Its mother's most unnatural bearing-bed.
Nor did she not bewail that nuptial-couch
Where she brought forth, unhappy, brood on brood,
Spouse to her spouse, and children to her child.
And then—I know no further how she perished;
For Oedipus brake in, crying aloud;
For whom it was impossible to watch
The ending of her misery; but on him
We gazed, as he went raging all about,
Beseeching us to furnish him a sword
And say where he could find his wife—no wife,
Rather the mother-soil both of himself
And children; and, as he raved thus, some Power
Shews him—at least, none of us present did.
Then, shouting loud, he sprang upon the doors
As following some guide, and burst the bars
Out of their sockets, and alights within.
There we beheld his wife hanging, entwined
In a twined noose. He seeing her, with a groan
Looses the halter; then, when on the ground
Lay the poor wretch, dreadful it was to see
What followed; snatching from her dress gold pins
Wherewith she was adorned, he lifted them,
And smote the nerves of his own eyeballs, saying
Something like this—that they should see no more
Evils like those he had endured or wrought;
Darkling, thereafter, let them gaze on forms
He might not see, and fail to recognize
The faces he desired! Chanting this burden,
Not once, but many times, he raised his hand
And stabbed his eyes; so that from both of them
The blood ran down his face, not drop by drop,
But all at once, in a dark shower of gore.
—These are the ills that from a two-fold source,
Not one alone, but in both wife and spouse,
Mingled together, have burst forth at once.

Their former pristine happiness indeed
Was happiness before; but in this hour
Shame—lamentation—Atè*—death—of all
That has a name of evil, nought's away!

1 SENATOR   And does he stand in any respite now
Of misery, poor soul?

2 MESSENGER   He calls aloud
For some one to undo the bolts, and shew
To all the Cadmeans him, his father's slayer—
His mother's—uttering words unhallowed—words
I may not speak; that he will cast himself
Forth of the land, abide no more at home
Under the curse of his own cursing. Nay,
But he lacks force, and guidance; for his sickness
Is more than man can bear. See for yourself;
For these gates open, and you will straight behold
A sight—such as even he that loathes must pity!

Enter OEDIPUS *blind*.

Chorus.

O sorrow, lamentable for eyes to see!
Sorest of all past ills encountering me!
What frenzy, O wretch, is this, that came on thee?

What Deity was it that with a leap so great—
Farther than farthest—sprang on thy sad fate?
Woe is me, woe is me for thee—unfortunate!

Fain would I gaze at thee, would ask thee much,
Many things learn of thee, wert thou not such
As I may not even behold, as I shudder to touch.

OEDIPUS   Me miserable! Whither must I go?
Ah whither flits my voice, borne to and fro?
Thou Power unseen, how hast thou brought me low!

* Doom caused by guilt and ignorance.

1 SENATOR   To ills, intolerable to hear or see.

OEDIPUS   Thou horror of thick darkness overspread,
      Thou shadow of unutterable dread
      Not to be stemmed or stayed, fallen on my head—

          Woe's me once more! How crowd upon my heart
            Stings of these wounds, and memories of woe!

1 SENATOR   No marvel if thou bear a double smart
          And writhe, so stricken, with a two-fold throe!

OEDIPUS   Still art thou near me—ready still to tend
      And to endure me, faithful to the end,
      Blind as I am, with kindness, O my friend!

          For strange thou art not; but full well I know
           That voice of thine, all darkling though I be.

1 SENATOR   Rash man, how could'st thou bear to outrage so
          Thine eyes? What Power was it, that wrought on thee?

OEDIPUS   Apollo, Apollo fulfils,
      O friends, my measure of ills—
      Fills my measure of woe;
      Author was none, but I,
      None other, of the blow;
      For why was I to see,
          When to descry
  No sight on earth could have a charm for me?

1 SENATOR   It was even as thou sayest.

OEDIPUS   What was there left for sight?
      What, that could give delight?
          Or whose address,
  O friends, could I still hear with happiness?
      Lead me to exile straight;
      Lead me, O my friends, the worst

Of murderers, of mortals most accurst,
      Yea and to Gods chief object of their hate.

1 SENATOR   Of cunning hapless, as of hapless fate,
      I would that I had never known thy name!

OEDIPUS   May he perish, whoe'er 'twas drew me
            Out of the cruel gyve
            That bound my feet, on the lea!
            He who saved me alive,
            Who rescued me from fate,
            Shewing no kindness to me!
                  Sorrow so great,
      Had I died then, had spared both mine and me.

1 SENATOR   Fain were I too it had been so.

OEDIPUS   Not then had I become
            My father's murderer,
      Nor wedded her I have my being from:
            Whom now no God will bless,
            Child of incestuousness
      In her that bare me, being the spouse of her;
      Yea if aught ill worse than all ill be there,
            That Oedipus must bear.

1 SENATOR   I know not how to say thou hast done well;
      For it were better for thee now to die,
      Than to live on in blindness.

OEDIPUS   Tell me not—
            Give me no counsel now, that what is done
            Has not been done thus best. I know not how
            With seeing eyes I could have looked upon
            My father—coming to the under-world,
            Or my poor mother, when against them both
            I have sinned sins, worse than a halter's meed.
            Or do you think that children were a sight
            Delectable for me to gaze at, born

As they were born? Never with eyes of mine!
No, nor the city, nor the citadel,
Nor consecrated shrines of deities,
From which, to my most utter misery,
I, of all other men in Thebes the man
Most bravely nurtured, cut myself away,
And of my own mouth dictated to all
To thrust out me, the impious—me, declared
Abominable of Heaven, and Laius' son.
Was I, who in myself made evident
So dark a stain, with unaverted eyes
To look on these? That least of all! Nay rather,
If there were any way to choke the fount
Of hearing, through my ears, I would have tried
To seal up all this miserable frame
And live blind, deaf to all things; sweet it were
To dwell in fancy, out of reach of pain.
—Cithaeron! wherefore didst thou harbour me!
Why not at once have slain me? Never then
Had I displayed before the face of men
Who and from whom I am! O Polybus,
And Corinth, and the old paternal roof
I once called mine, with what thin film of honour,
Corruption over-skinned, you fostered me,
Found ill myself, and from ill parents, now!
O you, the three roads, and the lonely brake,
The copse, and pass at the divided way,
Which at my hands drank blood that was my own—
My father's—do you keep in memory
What in your sight I did, and how again
I wrought, when I came hither? Wedlock, wedlock,
You gave me being, you raised up seed again
To the same lineage, and exhibited
In one incestuous flesh son—brother—sire,
Bride, wife and mother; and all ghastliest deeds
Wrought among men! But O, ill done, ill worded!

In Heaven's name hide me with all speed away,
Or slay me, or send adrift upon some sea
Where you may look on me no longer! Come,
Touch, if you will, a miserable man;
Pray you, fear nothing; for my misery
No mortal but myself can underbear.

1 SENATOR   Creon is at hand; he is the man you need,
Who must decide and do; being, after you,
The sole protector left us, for the land.

OEDIPUS   Ah Heaven, what language shall I hold to him?
What rightful credit will appear in me?
For I have been found wholly in the wrong
In all that passed between us heretofore!

Enter CREON.

CREON   Not as a mocker come I, Oedipus,
Nor to reproach for any former pain.
But you—even if you reverence no more
Children of men,—at least so far revere
The royal Sun-god's all-sustaining fire,
Not to parade, thus flagrant, such a sore
As neither earth nor day can tolerate,
Nor dew from Heaven! Take him in instantly!
That kindred only should behold and hear
The griefs of kin, fits best with decency.

OEDIPUS   In Heaven's name, seeing that you transported me
Beyond all hope, coming, the first of men,
To me the last of men, grant me one boon!
'Tis for your good, not for my own, I say it.

CREON   What is it that you crave so eagerly?

OEDIPUS   Out of this country cast me with all speed,
Where I may pass without accost of men.

CREON   So had I done, be sure, had I not wished
To learn our duty, first, at the God's mouth.

OEDIPUS   Surely his oracle was all made plain,
Me, the profane, the parricide, to slay!

CREON   So was it said; but in our present need
    'Tis better to enquire what we must do.
OEDIPUS   Will ye seek answer for a wretch like me?
CREON   Even you might trust what the God answers, now.
OEDIPUS   Ay, and I charge thee, and will beg of thee,
    Order thyself such burial as thou wilt,
    For her who lies within; seeing it is meet
    Thou do so, for thine own. But never more
    Be this my native town burdened with me
    For living inmate; rather suffer me
    To haunt the mountains—where my mountain is,
    Cithaeron, which my mother and my sire,
    Living, appointed for my sepulchre,
    That as they meant, my slayers, I may expire.
    Howbeit this much I know, neither disease
    Nor aught beside can kill me; never else
    Had I been rescued from the brink of death,
    But for some dire calamity. Ah well,
    Let our own fate wag onward as it may;
    And for my sons, Creon, take thou no care
    Upon thee; they are men, so that they never
    Can lack the means to live, where'er they be;
    But my two girls, wretched and pitiable,
    For whose repast was never board of mine
    Ordered apart, without me, but in all
    That I partook they always shared with me,
    Take care of them; and let me, above all else,
    Touch them with hands, and weep away my troubles!
    Pardon, my lord; pardon, illustrious sir;
    If but my hands could feel them, I might seem
    To have them still, as when I still could see.

ANTIGONE *and* ISMENE *are brought in.*

    —What do I say? In Heaven's name, do I not
    Hear my two darlings, somewhere shedding tears?
    And can it be that Creon, pitying me,

Sends me my dearest, my two daughters, hither?
Is it so indeed?

CREON   Yes, it is I vouchsafed this boon, aware
What joy you have and long have had of them.

OEDIPUS   Why then, good luck go with thee, and Providence
Be guardian to thee, better than to me,
In payment for their coming!—Children dear,
Where are you? Come, come hither to my arms—
To these brotherly arms—procurers that
The eyes—that were your sire's—once bright—should see
Thus! who am shewn, O children, to have been
Author of you—unseeing—unknowing—in
Her bed, whence I derived my being! You
I weep for; for I cannot gaze on you;
Knowing what is left of bitter in the life
Which at men's hands you needs must henceforth live.
For to what gatherings of the citizens
Will you resort, or to what festivals,
Whence you will not, in place of holiday,
Come home in tears? Or when you shall have grown
To years of marriage, who—ah, who will be
The man to abide the hazard of disgrace
Such as must be the bane, both of my sons,
And you as well? For what reproach is lacking?
Your father slew his father, and became
Father of you—by her who bare him. So
Will they reproach you; who will wed you then?
No one, my children; but you needs must wither,
Barren—unwed. But thou, Menoeceus' son,
Since thou art all the father these have left them,
For we, the two that were their parents, now
Are both undone, do not thou suffer them
To wander, vagabond and husband-less,
Being of thy kin; nor let them fall so low
As are my fortunes; but have pity on them,
Seeing them so tender, and so desolate

Of all friends, but for thee. Give me thy hand,
Good sir, and promise this.—To you, my girls,
If you were old enough to understand,
I should have much to say; but as it is,
This be your prayer; in some permitted place
That you may breathe; and have your lot in life
Happier than his, who did engender you.

CREON Get thee in; thou hast bewailed thee enough, in reason.

OEDIPUS Though it be bitter, I must do it.

CREON   All's good, in good season.

OEDIPUS Do you know how to make me?

CREON   Say on, and I shall know.

OEDIPUS Banish me from this country.

CREON   That must the God bestow.

OEDIPUS But to Gods, above all men, I am a mark for hate.

CREON And for that same reason you will obtain it straight.

OEDIPUS Say you so?

CREON   Yes truly, and I mean what I say.

OEDIPUS Lead me hence then, quickly.

CREON   Go; but let the children stay.

OEDIPUS Do not take them from me!

CREON   Think not to have all at thy pleasure;
For what thou didst attain to far outwent thy measure.

CREON, *the Children, etc. retire.*   OEDIPUS *is led in.*

Chorus.

Dwellers in Thebes, behold this Oedipus,
The man who solved the riddle marvellous,
A prince of men,
Whose lot what citizen
Did not with envy see,
How deep the billows of calamity
        Above him roll.

Watch therefore and regard that supreme day;
And of no mortal say
"That man is happy," till
Vexed by no grievous ill
    He pass Life's goal.

[Exeunt omnes.

Oedipus at Colonus

Oedipus at Colonus was, as far as we know, the last play Sophocles wrote; it was first produced, by his son, several years following his death.

Although relatively little is known of Sophocles' life, we do know that he was born in Colonus and was a prominent citizen of Athens for most of his long life. There is a special poignancy, then, to this play. It paints a restrained but heartfelt portrait of Athens, its people, and its ruler, who, despite initial misgivings, show great fair-mindedness, integrity, and empathy in their dealings with the figure of Oedipus—a forbidding and difficult presence, at best, in this drama. This portrait may well have represented Sophocles' last public tribute to the city, the civilization, to which he was so dedicated. In addition, the play's setting, Colonus—the spot where Oedipus's sufferings will come to an end, where he is to willingly obey the will of the gods, and the spot which the oracles have told him will be protected henceforth, once he chooses it for his burial ground—may well capture the great tragedian's own wish to bestow a final blessing on his birthplace.

JULIE NORD

Persons Represented

ŒDIPUS.

ANTIGONE,
ISMENE, } *his daughters.*

THESEUS, *king of Athens.*

CREON.

POLYNICES, *son to Œdipus.*

A *Stranger, an inhabitant of Colonus.*

A *Messenger, an Athenian attending on Theseus.*

The CHORUS *is composed of citizens of Colonus.*
Guards attending on Theseus and Creon.
An attendant following Ismene.

Oedipus at Colonus

Scene—Colonus, before the Sacred Grove of the Erinyes.

[*Enter* ŒDIPUS *and* ANTIGONE.]

ŒDIPUS Antigone, child of a blind old man,
        What lands are these, or what the folk whose gates
        We have attained? Who shall receive to-day
        With stinted alms the wanderer Œdipus?—
        Asking but little; than that little still
        Obtaining less; and yet enough for me.
        For my afflictions and the weight of years
        And something, too, of my own dignity
        Teach me contentment. If you see, my child,
        Some resting-place, either by sacred grove
        Or secular dwelling, stay me and set me down,
        That we may find out in what place we are;
        For strangers from inhabitants to learn
        We are come hither; and what we hear, to do it.
ANTIGONE Towers are there, O my father, Œdipus,
        Covering a city, I perceive, afar;
        This place, as I suppose, is consecrate;
        It blooms with laurel, olive and the vine;[1]
        Thick-flying nightingales within it warble;
        Here stretch thy limbs, upon this rough-hewn stone;
        For thou art aged to have come so far.

---

[1]The laurel is sacred to Apollo, the olive to Athena, and the vine to Dionysus. The presence of these things therefore demonstrates the sacred nature of the spot. Nightingales may have indicated, in addition, the presence of Pan.

ŒDIPUS   Seat me and guard me still; for I am blind.
ANTIGONE   I know—that is an old tale—tell not me.
ŒDIPUS   Well, can you teach me whither we are come?
ANTIGONE   To Athens, that I know; but not the quarter.
ŒDIPUS   So much we heard from every passenger.
ANTIGONE   But shall I go and ask what place it is?
ŒDIPUS   Why yes, my child; if it seems hospitable.
ANTIGONE   O yes, there are some dwellings.—There's no need,
          I think: for here's a man, I see, close to us.
ŒDIPUS   What, moving and approaching hitherward?
ANTIGONE   Yes, here, I mean, at hand. Say what is needful;
          This is the man.

          [*Enter a Stranger, an inhabitant of Colonus.*]

ŒDIPUS   Stranger, this maiden tells me
          (Whose eyesight serves both for herself and me)
          Of your approach, an apt intelligencer
          Of things we cannot guess—
STRANGER   Ere you ask further
          Come from that seat; you trespass on a place
          No foot may desecrate.
ŒDIPUS   What is the place?
          To what God dedicated?
STRANGER   It is kept
          From touch or dwelling: the dread Goddesses
          Hold it, the daughters of the Earth and Gloom.
ŒDIPUS   Who? By what solemn name denominate
          Might I invoke them?
STRANGER   By the natives here
          They would be called the All-seeing Favourers;
          Other fit names elsewhere.
ŒDIPUS   May they receive
          With mercy me their supplicant; and I
          From this land's harbour will go forth no more!
STRANGER   What does this mean?
ŒDIPUS   'Tis my misfortunes' weird.
STRANGER   Truly I dare not turn him out, before
          I tell the rest—without authority.
ŒDIPUS   Sir, in Heaven's name do not begrudge me—me
          A wanderer—what I crave of you to say!
STRANGER   Explain, and I will show I grudge you not.
ŒDIPUS   What ground is this we have been treading on?

STRANGER   You shall hear all I know. First the whole place is holy,
        Inhabited by dread Poseidon;[2] next
        The Deity that brought fire abides in it,
        Titan Prometheus;[3] this same spot you press
        They call the Brass-paved Causeway[4] of the land—
        Rampart of Athens; the adjoining farms
        Boast them Colonus[5] mounted on his horse
        For their chief patron, and the people all
        Are called by and in common bear his name.
        These are the facts, sir stranger; honoured not
        So much in story, as cherished on the spot.
ŒDIPUS   Did you say any men lived hereabouts?
STRANGER   Yes truly, and that they bear this Hero's name.
ŒDIPUS   Have they a chief, or lies it with the folk
        To hold debate?
STRANGER   These parts are in the rule
        Of the king of the City.
ŒDIPUS   Who is he whose might
        And counsel sway them?
STRANGER   Theseus is his name,
        Old Ægeus' son.
ŒDIPUS   Would one of you go fetch him?
STRANGER   What should one tell or move him to come here for?
ŒDIPUS   Say, to gain much by a small act of kindness.
STRANGER   And where's the service in a man that's blind?
ŒDIPUS   There will be eyes in all that I shall say.
STRANGER   Come, this you may, sir, and without offence;
        (Since you are worshipful to look upon,
        Saving God's hand;) stay there where I first found you,
        While I go tell this to the burghers round,
        (Here, not in the city;) they will soon decide
        If you shall tarry, or depart once more.   [*Exit.*
ŒDIPUS   My daughter, has the stranger gone away?
ANTIGONE   Yes, he has gone. You may say anything
        Securely, father; none are here but I.
ŒDIPUS   Queens, with stern faces! since of all this land
        First in your sanctuary I seated me,

[2]*Poseidon*] God of the sea.
[3]*Prometheus*] The god who gave fire to humankind; he was punished by Zeus but the
   Greeks considered him to be perhaps their greatest ally amongst the gods.
[4]*Brass-paved Causeway*] The dread pathway to Hades (elsewhere called the "Brazen
   stairs").
[5]*Colonus*] Nothing is known of this hero, for whom the town is named.

To Phœbus,[6] as to me, turn no deaf ear,
Who, prophesying of those my many woes,
Spake of this respite for me at the last
That when my journey ended, in a land
Where I should find asylum, at the shrine
Of awful Powers, and hospitality,
There I should round the goal of my life-sorrow,
There dwell, a blessing to my hosts—a curse
To those who sent me into banishment;
Giving me rede a sign of this should come,
In earthquake, thunder, or lightning out of heaven.
Now I perceive it is from none but you,
The faithful omen that has guided me
Along my pathway hither to this grove.
Else I should never in my wayfaring
Have met you first so fitly—strangers you
To wine,[7] as I am—or have taken seat
Upon this awful footstone, all unhewn.
Now therefore, Goddesses, bestow on me,
According to Apollo's oracle,
Some passing, some quick finish of my life;
If I appear not still unperfected
In my continual servitude of toils,
The extremest mortals know. Come, you kind daughters
Of ancient Gloom! Come, thou that bear'st the name
Of mightiest Pallas,[8] Athens, first of cities,
Have pity upon this miserable ghost
Of what was Œdipus! He is not now
Such as of old.

ANTIGONE   Hush! there are people coming,
Elders in years, who note you where you sit.

ŒDIPUS   I will be silent, and do you conceal me
Apart within the grove, till I may learn
What language these men hold; for in the knowledge
Prudence consists for what we have to do.

[*ŒDIPUS and* ANTIGONE *retire.*]

[*Enter Citizens of Colonus, as Chorus.*]

[6]*Phoebus*] Apollo, god of light and truth. It was his oracle (at Delphi) that prophesied
  Oedipus' crimes and subsequent fate.
[7]*strangers you to wine*] It was forbidden to pour wine as libation to the Eumenides, the
  "Queens, with stern faces" to whom Oedipus speaks.
[8]*Pallas*] Athena, goddess of wisdom.

Chorus

Look! Who was it? Where abides he?
In what nook or corner hides he—
Of all men—of all mankind the most presuming?
Search about. Spy him, there!
Seek him out everywhere.
A vagrant—some vagrant the grey-beard must have been
None of our countrymen.
Otherwise he never would have dreamt of coming
To the untrodden thicket of the Virgins here,
Of the mighty Powers, whom to name we fear,
Whose abode we pass unprying,
Without babble or loud crying,
Keeping mouth closely pent
Save on what is innocent.
Now, 'tis said, void of dread,
Some one has intruded on the sacred space;
I the bound searching round
Cannot yet alight upon his hiding place.

ŒDIPUS   [*advancing, with* ANTIGONE] I am the man; for by the sound
     I see you,
   As is the saying.
1 CITIZEN   Hilloa! hoa! who is this,
   Dreadful to see, dreadful to hear?
ŒDIPUS   I pray you,
   Do not regard me as a trespasser—
1 CITIZEN   Averting Jove! who may this old man be?
ŒDIPUS   One of a sort far other than the first
   To be deemed happy, O you guardians
   Over this land; I am myself the proof;
   I should not otherwise be groping thus,
   Led by another's eyesight, or, being great,
   On slender moorings come to anchorage.

Chorus

Eh thine eyes! thy blind eyes!
Wert thou thus, as I surmise,
For sad life—for long life—equipped from life's beginning?
None the more, if so be,
Shalt thou score, spite of me,

On curses fresh curses, by sinning—yea, by sinning.
   But that thou trespass not
On the grassy coverts of this hallowed spot,
Where the bowl of water by the herbage quaffed
Flows with mingled runnels of a sweetened draught—
  Beware, beware sirrah stranger!
  Get thee hence! Avoid thy danger!
   (His long start costs me dear);
   Thou tired vagabond, dost hear?
   Though thou bring word or thing
Hither for debate, avoid the sacred glen!
   Passing where all may fare
Speak with freedom; but refrain thee, until then!

ŒDIPUS Daughter, what course is to be thought of, now?
ANTIGONE My father, what the citizens observe
  That should we also; yield in what we must,
  And hearken.
ŒDIPUS   Well, give me a hand.
ANTIGONE   You have it.
ŒDIPUS Sirs, let me meet no wrong, if I remove
  Trusting in you.
CITIZEN   Never against thy will
  Out of these sanctuaries, ancient sir,
  Shall any drag thee.
ŒDIPUS   Am I to proceed?
1 CITIZEN Yes, further yet.
ŒDIPUS   Still further?
1 CITIZEN   Damsel, lead,
  And bring him further on; for you perceive.
ANTIGONE Follow, my father, follow in my train,
  With feet all darkling.
1 CITIZEN   Man of woes, endure,
  Being as thou art, a stranger on strange soil,
  To abhor whate'er the City has held in hate,
  And what She loves, to honour.
ŒDIPUS   Come, my child,
  Lead me where, stepping without sacrilege,
  Something we may impart, something receive;
  And let us not contend with fate.
1 CITIZEN   Halt there!
  No further bend thy steps, over that ramp
  Of rock in front.

ŒDIPUS   What, thus?
1 CITIZEN   Yes, as you have it.
ŒDIPUS   May I be seated?
1 CITIZEN   Yes, if you bend sideways,
     And sit down low, just on the edge of the stone.
ANTIGONE   Father, this is my office; gently take
     One step with my step, and commit—
ŒDIPUS   Eh me!
ANTIGONE   Thine aged frame to loving hand of mine.
ŒDIPUS   [seated] Ah, my misfortune!
1 CITIZEN   Man of woes, declare
     (Now that thou art at ease) what was thy birth,
     What toil-worn wanderer thou art, what country
     We are to know for thine.
ŒDIPUS   Ah strangers,
     I am an outcast; but forbear, forbear—
1 CITIZEN   Why do you put this matter from you, sir?
ŒDIPUS   Forbear, I say, to ask me what I am,
     Nor seek nor question further.
1 CITIZEN   Wherefore so?
ŒDIPUS   Awful my birth.
1 CITIZEN   Tell it.
ŒDIPUS   O child—ah me,
     What must I answer?
1 CITIZEN   Of what seed thou art
     Of the father's side, sir, say.
ŒDIPUS   Woe's me, my child,
     What will become of me?
ANTIGONE   Speak, for you tread
     The very verge.
ŒDIPUS   I will; I have no refuge.
1 CITIZEN   Ye are both long about it; make more speed!
ŒDIPUS   Know ye of one from Laius—
1 CITIZEN   Ha, how? how?
ŒDIPUS   And of the race of Labdacus—
1 CITIZEN   O Jove!
ŒDIPUS   Miserable Œdipus?
1 CITIZEN   And art thou he?
ŒDIPUS   Have ye no fear at what I say—
CITIZENS   Oh! oh!
ŒDIPUS   Unhappy!
CITIZENS   Out, O out!

ŒDIPUS   Now, daughter,
    What must we look for next?
CITIZENS   Off, off,
    Out of the place!
ŒDIPUS   And what you promised me,
    What will you make of that?

Chorus

    No retribution hath Fortune in store
    For the man who requites what he suffered before;
    Treason, by treason withstood, and surpassed,
    Pays a man trouble, not favour, at last.
    Now back with you, back! You have sailing orders.
    Get out of this place! Go forth from our borders!
    Bring to our gates no more evil fates!
ANTIGONE   Pious strangers,
        Although you brook not
    The old man's presence, my father, here,
        To what he did
        (Though not with purpose)
    Listening, lending an open ear,
    Me, not the less, poor maid, I entreat,
    Pity, O strangers, who fall at your feet—
    Fall at your feet, for my father's sake only
      With eyes unblasted facing your face,
      Even as though born one of your race,
    So mercy may light on the helpless and lonely!
    On you, as on Heaven, we depend; reject not
    The prayer of the poor, for grace we expect not.
    By all you hold dear as your own heart's blood!
    By your brood! By your bed! By your need! By your God!
    You will find no man, searching with heed,
    But he must follow, if God lead.

1 CITIZEN   Daughter of Œdipus, both him and you,
    Trust us, we pity alike, in your distress;
    But, reverencing Heaven, we have no power
    To go beyond what has been told you now.
ŒDIPUS   What is the use of reputation, then,
    Or what of good report, flowing all to nothing,
    If it be said of Athens, that she is
    The most religious and the only state
    Able to guard the stranger in distress,

And that she only can suffice his need,
While you—to me—what have you done with it?
Who from these steps dislodged me, and then, in fear
Of my name, merely, are expelling me;
For of my person it is not, or my deeds;
The things I did were rather done to me—
If I must speak of that my parentage,
For which, as well I know, you are scared at me.
And after all, where was my villainy?
I but requited evil done to me;
So that, although I did it knowingly,
Not even then should I be proved a villain.
But as it is, I went the way I went
Unwittingly; and suffered at the hands
Of those who knew that they were injuring me.
Wherefore in Heaven's name I beseech you, sirs,
Even as you raised me from my seat, now save me,
And do not, in your reverence for Gods,
Make nought of the Gods' dues; rather consider
How that they mark the virtuous among men,
And mark the wicked too; and that escape
Was never yet, of any man profane.
In whose obedience tarnish not the fame
Of Athens the august, lending your hand
To any act of profanation. No!
As you received the suppliant, on your promise,
So rescue and preserve me; and survey
These brows, of ill aspect, not without honour.
For holy and righteous am I, who come hither,
And I bring profit to these citizens;
And when that lord arrives, who is your leader,
If you will hearken, I will tell you all;
In the mean time see that you deal not falsely.

1 CITIZEN   We needs must feel a certain awe, old man,
　　　　At that which you suggest; for it is couched
　　　　In words of no light weight. Sufficeth us
　　　　That the land's rulers should decide the case.

ŒDIPUS   And where is he who rules this country, sirs?

1 CITIZEN   He keeps his father's hold, here; but a post,
　　　　The same who sent me hither, is gone to fetch him.

ŒDIPUS   Do you suppose he will give heed, or take,
　　　　For a blind man, the trouble to draw near?

1 CITIZEN   Ay truly, when he hears your name.

ŒDIPUS   But who
    Is there to tell him that?
1 CITIZEN   'Tis a long way;
    But travellers' gossip often gets abroad,
    Which when he hears, he will come, never fear.
    For far and wide, old man, has your name travelled;
    So that, although he sleep, and tarry long,
    Hearing of you, he will make haste and come.
ŒDIPUS   I wish he may, for his own city's good
    And mine. For who does not befriend himself
    By doing good?
ANTIGONE   O Jove, what shall I say?
    What shall I think, my father?
ŒDIPUS   But what is it,
    Antigone, my child?
ANTIGONE   I see a woman
    Coming toward us, mounted on a horse
    Of Ætnean breed; and a Thessalian bonnet
    Is on her head, tied close about her face,
    To screen it from the sun. What shall I say?
    Is it—or not? or do my thoughts mislead?
    Yes! No! I know not what to say. Alack,
    It is no other. Yes, and she looks joyful
    At spying me, as she draws near, and shews
    It is no other than Ismene's self!
ŒDIPUS   How say you, child?
ANTIGONE   Why, that I see your child,
    My sister; you can tell her by the voice.

[*Enter* ISMENE *and attendant.*]

ISMENE   Father—and sister! the two names to me
    That are most dear! How hardly have I found you,
    And hardly can regard you now, for grief!
ŒDIPUS   O child, are you come hither?
ISMENE   O my father,
    Hapless to look on!
ŒDIPUS   Are you here, my child?
ISMENE   After much trouble, yes.
ŒDIPUS   Touch me, my girl.
ISMENE   I touch you, both of you.
ŒDIPUS   Offspring of mine—
    Sisters—

ISMENE   Alas, what miseries—
ŒDIPUS   Hers and mine?
ISMENE   Yes, and my own, wretch that I am!
ŒDIPUS   My child,
        Why did you come?
ISMENE   Father, in care for you.
ŒDIPUS   You wanted me?
ISMENE   Yes, and to bring you news
        In person, with my one true servant here.
ŒDIPUS   And the young men your brothers, where have they
        Bestowed their labour?
ISMENE   They are—where they are;
        It is a heavy time with them, just now.
ŒDIPUS   O how exactly fitted are that pair,
        In character and training, for the ways
        Followed in Egypt! For the husbands there
        Sit within walls and weave, while out of doors
        Their partners fare, winning their daily food.
        Even so, my children, they who fittingly
        Should bear this burden which you bear, like maidens
        Keep house at home, while in their stead you two
        Are toiling to relieve my miseries.
        One, from the time she left her nursery
        And grew to her full strength, in my train ever
        Wanders in wretchedness, an old man's leader,
        Through the wild forest often journeying
        Foodless and footsore, toiling painfully
        Often—in rain and the sun's sultriness,
        Holding the comforts of her life at home
        As nothing, to the tending of her sire.
        While you, my child, sallied out once before
        Bringing your father all the oracles
        That were delivered as concerning me,
        Without the Cadmeans' knowledge, and became
        My faithful watcher, when they banished me;
        And now again—what story are you come
        To tell your father? what dispatch, Ismene,
        Transported you from home? for you are come
        Not empty, at least; of that I am assured;
        Nor without bringing me some cause for fear.
ISMENE   What sufferings, my father, I endured,
        Seeking your lodging and abiding-place,
        I will pass over; for I do not care

>   To feel the pain twice over, in the travail,
>   And after, in the telling. But the ills
>   Now compassing your two unhappy sons—
>   These I have come to shew. For formerly
>   They were both eager that the sovereignty
>   Should pass to Creon, and the city, so,
>   Not be defiled; professing to regard
>   The inveterate perdition of the race,
>   Such as had fastened on your woeful house;
>   But now some God, and an infatuate mind,
>   Has caused an evil struggle to arise
>   Between that pair, thrice miserable, to seize
>   Upon the government and royal power.
>   And now the lad, the younger of the twain,
>   Is robbing Polynices of the throne,
>   Who is his elder, and has driven him forth
>   Out of his native land. He, taking flight
>   (As is the general rumour in our ears)
>   To Argos in the Vale, is gaining there
>   New comrades and connexions to his side,
>   Swearing that Argos either shall forthwith
>   Humble the glory of the Cadmeans' land,[9]
>   Or else, exalt it to the height of heaven.
>   Dear father, this is not a wordy tale;
>   'Tis dreadful fact; and at what point the Gods
>   Mean to take pity upon your woes, I know not.

ŒDIPUS   And did you hope already that the Gods
        Would have some care for my deliverance?

ISMENE   Yes, father, after this new oracle.

ŒDIPUS   What is it? What has been revealed, my child?

ISMENE   That you shall be by the inhabitants
        Sought to hereafter, for their safety's sake,
        Whether in life or death.

ŒDIPUS   But who could profit
        By such as I?

ISMENE   On you, 'tis said, their power
        Comes to depend.

ŒDIPUS   What, now my life is finished,
        Do I begin to live?

---

[9]Cadmus was the acknowledged founder of Thebes. The city's people, therefore, bear his name.

ISMENE   'Tis the Gods, now,
    Uplift you, who destroyed you formerly.
ŒDIPUS   To fall when young, and be set up when old,
    Is poor exchange!
ISMENE   And on this errand know
    That Creon will be here, and that ere long.
ŒDIPUS   With what intent, my daughter? Construe me.
ISMENE   To lodge you in the parts near Cadmean soil,
    So they may have you in their power, but you
    Never set foot within its boundaries.
ŒDIPUS   How are they helped by my lying at their doors?
ISMENE   Your being buried inauspiciously
    Brings them disaster.
ŒDIPUS   Even without a God
    One might conclude so far.
ISMENE   Therefore they seek
    To attach you, near their land, where you may be
    No longer your own master.
ŒDIPUS   Do they mean
    To shroud me in the dust of Thebes?
ISMENE   Nay, father,
    Taint of a kinsman's blood forbids it you.
ŒDIPUS   Then they shall never get me in their power.
ISMENE   That will go hard with men of Thebes one day.
ŒDIPUS   How should that be, my child?
ISMENE   Through wrath of yours,
    When they approach your grave.
ŒDIPUS   Child—what you say—
    Whence did you hear it all?
ISMENE   From envoys sent
    To inquire at Delphi's shrine.
ŒDIPUS   Was Phœbus he
    Who hath said these things of me?
ISMENE   So they report
    Who came to Thebes.
ŒDIPUS   Did either of my sons
    Hear it?
ISMENE   Yes, both alike, and well they know it.
ŒDIPUS   And did the varlets, when they heard it, still
    Prefer their kingship to regard for me?
ISMENE   I grieve to hear the question; all the same,
    Such is my news.

ŒDIPUS   Then may the Gods not quench
    The fated strife betwixt them, and the end
    May it be for me to give them, of that battle
    On which they are set, levelling their spear-points now!
    So neither shall that one of them abide
    Who holds the sceptre now, and throne, nor he
    Who has departed ever more return:
    Who verily, when I who fathered them
    Was thrust out of the land so shamefully,
    Stayed not nor screened me; but between them I
    Was sent adrift, sentenced to banishment.
    "A favour," you may say, "the city then
    Granted me, as of course, at my desire";
    Nay truly! for upon that selfsame day
    When my brain boiled, and to be stoned and die
    Seemed sweetest, there was no one that stood up
    To help me to my craving; but long after,
    When all the trouble was no longer green,
    And I perceived my passion had outstripped
    The chastisement of my offences past,
    Then was it that this happened; then the city
    Violently drave me from the land, at last;
    While they, their father's offspring, in whose power
    It lay to help their father, would not do it,
    But I have had to wander, out and on,
    Thanks to the little word they would not say,
    In beggary and exile. And from these,
    Being maidens, all that nature lends to them,
    Both sustenance and safety by the way,
    Ay and familiar comfort, I receive;
    While they preferred to their own father thrones
    And sceptred rule and territorial sway.
    But me for an ally they shall not gain;
    Nor ever from their Cadmean monarchy
    Shall benefit flow to them; this I know,
    Hearing the oracle she brings me now,
    And minding, too, that ancient prophecy
    Of mine, by Phœbus brought to pass on me.
    So now let them send Creon after me,
    And every lusty catch-poll in their town;
    For, gentlemen, if in the train of these,
    The awful Powers who guard your village-ground,
    You shall decide to summon up your force

In my behalf, then will you, for this city,
Procure a mighty saviour, and entail
Troubles on those, who are my enemies.

1 CITIZEN   First, you have won our pity, Œdipus,
Both for yourself and for your daughters; next,
Seeing that beside this pleading you propose
Yourself, to be a saviour for our land,
I am disposed to give you some good counsel.

ŒDIPUS   Stand my friend, most kind sir; and I will do
All that you bid me.

1 CITIZEN .   Come and institute
Rites of purgation to the deities
Whose ground you trespassed on, when you came hither.

ŒDIPUS   After what fashion, sirs? instruct me.

1 CITIZEN   First
Bring holy water from a running stream;
But let your hands be pure.

ŒDIPUS   And afterward,
When I have drawn the limpid wave?

1 CITIZEN   There stand
Bowls, of an artist's carving; garland thou
Their rims, and the two ear-handles.

ŒDIPUS   With twigs,
Or bits of wool, or how?

1 CITIZEN   With a lock of wool,
New-shorn, ta'en from a yeanling ewe.

ŒDIPUS   So be it.
And after, how am I to make an end?

1 CITIZEN   Turn to the region where the dawn begins,
And pour libations.

ŒDIPUS   From the vessels, there,
Of which you spake, am I to pour them?

1 CITIZEN   Yes,
From each of three, one; and the last bowl drain.

ŒDIPUS   This last—how must I fill it, for the rite?
Tell me this too.

1 CITIZEN   With honey and water; add
No drop of wine.

ŒDIPUS   And when the bosky soil
Has taken these?

1 CITIZEN   Strew thrice nine olive-boughs
On either hand; and offer up this prayer.

ŒDIPUS   Ay, that is of most moment. Let me hear it.

1 CITIZEN   That as we call them Favourers, they would deign
             With favouring breasts to accept the supplicant,
             And save him; pray yourself, or in your stead
             Some other, speaking in an undertone,
             Not so as to be heard. Then come away
             And do not look behind you. This performed,
             I will stand by you gladly; otherwise,
             O stranger, I should have my fears for you.
ŒDIPUS   Girls, do you hear these people of the place?
ANTIGONE   We hear them well. Tell us what we must do.
ŒDIPUS   I cannot go; for neither have I strength
          Nor eyesight for the work—two hindrances;
          One of you two go and discharge this duty;
          For I suppose one spirit will suffice
          For tens of thousands, with good will, to do it.
          Make haste and set about it, anyhow;
          But do not leave me by myself alone;
          For in my frame there is not strength enough
          To creep unaided, or without a guide.
ISMENE   Well, I will go and do it. But the place—
          I want to know where I must look for it.
1 CITIZEN   Lady, beyond this thicket. Anything
             That you may need, there is one dwelling there
             Who will inform you.
ISMENE   I will betake me to it.
          Guard you our father here, Antigone.
          We may not take account of labour, even
          If we do labour, in a parent's cause.   [*Exit.*

I. 1.

1 CITIZEN   Stranger! 'Tis cruel to awake again
             The long since deadened pain;
             And yet I fain would learn—
ŒDIPUS   What is it, friend?
1 CITIZEN   The story of all that self-disclosed distress—
             Pitiful, remediless—
             Wherewith it was thy fortune to contend.
ŒDIPUS   Nay do not, for your hospitality,
          Open my ruthless wounds!
1 CITIZEN   I long to know,
             And to know right, that which is noised of thee
             So widely, and so unremittingly.

ŒDIPUS   Woe's me!
1 CITIZEN   Bear with me, I pray thee.
ŒDIPUS   Woe, ah woe!
1 CITIZEN   Hearken to my request;
        For I too hearken in all, at thy behest.

I. 2.

ŒDIPUS   Guilt overwhelmed me, friends—whelmed me, in sooth,
        (God be my witness!) undesigned, unsought;
        Nought was of purpose in the ills I wrought.
1 CITIZEN   To what effect?
ŒDIPUS   The city bound the chain
        Of an unhappy nuptial-bond on me,
        That knew not what I did.
1 CITIZEN   Didst thou in truth,
        As I hear said,
        Share an ill-omened bed
        With her—who was thy mother?
ŒDIPUS   O, I die,
        Stranger, to hear it uttered! And these twain—
1 CITIZEN   How say'st thou?
ŒDIPUS   Young
        Daughters of mine, twin curses!
1 CITIZEN   God!
ŒDIPUS   Are sprung
        From the same mother's travail-pangs, as I.

II. 1.

1 CITIZEN   Are these thy off-spring?
ŒDIPUS   Yes,
        And their sire's sisters also.
1 CITIZEN   Alas!
ŒDIPUS   Alas,
        Wave upon wave of evils, numberless!
1 CITIZEN   Thou didst endure—
ŒDIPUS   I endured misery;
        Yea, it abides with me.
1 CITIZEN   Thou didst commit—
ŒDIPUS   Nay, I committed nothing!
1 CITIZEN   How was that?
ŒDIPUS   I but received a boon, wretch that I was!

Such, that my service never merited at
The city's hands, to have the gift of it.

II. 2.

1 CITIZEN   How then, unhappy one? Wert thou the cause—
ŒDIPUS   What next? What wouldst thou know?
1 CITIZEN   Of thine own father's murder?
ŒDIPUS   O my heart!
    Thou hast struck me a second blow,
    Smart upon smart!
1 CITIZEN   Didst thou kill—
ŒDIPUS   Yea, I killed him. But the deed
    Had something in it—
1 CITIZEN   What is there to plead?
ŒDIPUS   Appealing to the laws.
1 CITIZEN   How could that be?
ŒDIPUS   I will declare to thee;
    Those whom I slew would have been slayers of me;
    Whence legally stainless, and in innocence,
    I stumbled on the offence.
1 CITIZEN   Here is our master Theseus, Ægeus' son,
    Come, at thy word, to do thine errand here.

[*Enter* THESEUS.]

THESEUS   Many aforetime having brought to me
    The bloody story of thine eyes put out,
    O son of Laius, I was ware of thee;
    And now, from rumour as I came along,
    I am the more assured; for by thy garb
    And thine afflicted presence we perceive
    That thou art really he; and pitying thee,
    Thou forlorn Œdipus, I would enquire
    With what petition to the city or me
    Thou and thy hapless follower wait on us?
    Instruct me; for calamitous indeed
    Must be the case disclosed by thee, wherefrom
    I should start backward; who remember well
    How in my youth I was a wanderer,
    Even as thy self; and strove with perils no less
    In my own person, on a foreign soil,
    Than any on earth; wherefore no foreigner,

Such as now thou art, would I turn aside
From helping to deliver; knowing well
That I am human, and have no more share
In what to-morrow will afford, than thou.

ŒDIPUS   Theseus, thy nobleness—without much talking—
Hath so vouchsafed, that little is required
For me to say. For thou hast named for me
Both who I am, and from what father sprung,
And from what country coming; wherefore now
Nothing is left me, but to speak the thing
Which I have need of, and my say is said.

THESEUS   That very thing now tell, that I may know it.

ŒDIPUS   I come, meaning to give this sorry body
A gift to thee; not goodly to the eyesight;
But better is the gain to come of it
Than beauty.

THESEUS   But what gain do you suppose
Your coming brings?

ŒDIPUS   In due time you will know;
Not just at present.

THESEUS   At what period
Will the advantage of your gift be shewn?

ŒDIPUS   When I am dead, and you have buried me.

THESEUS   O, you are claiming life's last offices;
But all that lies between—either you forget,
Or prize at nothing.

ŒDIPUS   Yes, because in them
I have all the rest summed up.

THESEUS   Tiny indeed
Is this request you proffer!

ŒDIPUS   No; look to it;
The coming struggle is not—is not light.

THESEUS   Do you speak of your own offspring and of me?

ŒDIPUS   King, they would fain convey me thither.

THESEUS   Well,
If you are not unwilling—to stay banished
Were hardly for your honour.

ŒDIPUS   When I wished it,
They were the hindrance!

THESEUS   O insensate one,
Wrath is not fitting in adversity!

ŒDIPUS   When you have heard me, censure; but as yet
Spare me.

THESEUS   Say on; for inconsiderately
          It fits me not to speak.

ŒDIPUS   Theseus, I have suffered
          Wrongs upon wrongs, most cruel.

THESEUS   Do you mean
          The old misfortune of your birth?

ŒDIPUS   O no;
          There is no Greek who does not babble of that!

THESEUS   What is this sickness then, of which you ail,
          Sorer than human?

ŒDIPUS   Thus it stands with me;
          By my own offspring was I hunted forth
          Out of my country; and I never more
          Can, as a parricide, again return.

THESEUS   Then why should they desire to send for you,
          To make you live remote?

ŒDIPUS   The divine lips
          Leave them no choice.

THESEUS   What sort of detriment
          Are they afraid of, from the oracles?

ŒDIPUS   It is their destiny to be overthrown
          Here, in this land.

THESEUS   And how shall come about
          The bitter feeling between them and me?

ŒDIPUS   Dear son of Ægeus, to the Gods alone
          Belongs it never to be old or die,
          But all things else melt with all-powerful Time.
          Earth's might decays, the body's might decays,
          And belief dies, and disbelief grows greenly;
          And varying ever is the passing breath
          Either 'twixt friend and friend, or city and city.
          For to some now, and by and by to some,
          Their friendship's pleasantness is turned to gall,
          Ay, and again to friendship. So in Thebes,
          Though all be now smooth weather there toward you,
          Yet, as he goes, the multitudinous Time
          Gives birth to multitudinous nights and days,
          Wherein, at a mere word, shall Theban steel
          Sever your now harmonious hand-claspings!
          Then shall my sleeping and invisible clay,
          Cold in the ground, drink their warm life-blood—if
          Jove be still Jove, and Jove-born Phœbus true.

But since it is unpleasing to declare.
The words that sleep unuttered, suffer me
To stay as I began, making but good
The pledge you gave; and you shall never say
(So but the Gods do not prove false to me)
That you received, into this land of yours,
In Œdipus, a thankless habitant.

1 CITIZEN   The man, my Liege, has constantly averred
             He will perform these and like offices
             Unto our land.

THESEUS   Who is there would reject
The tender of goodwill from such as he,
To whom, indeed, the hearth of comradeship
With us is ever open? and besides,
He, coming as a suppliant to the Gods,
Pays no small tribute to the land, and me.
Mindful whereof, I never will repel
The favour that he proffers; nay, I will
Replant him in our country. And if here
'Tis pleasant to the stranger to abide,
I shall enjoin you to take care of him;
Or if it pleases him to go with me—
Why, Œdipus, I leave to you the word,
Which you will choose. Your pleasure shall be mine.

ŒDIPUS   O Zeus, shower blessings on such men as this!
THESEUS   Which is your fancy? To go home with me?
ŒDIPUS   If it were lawful. But the spot is here—
THESEUS   For you to do—what? for I shall not hinder.
ŒDIPUS   For me to vanquish those who have banished me—
THESEUS   You magnify the advantage of your presence.
ŒDIPUS   If what you say abides, and you perform.
THESEUS   Be easy about me; I shall not fail you.
ŒDIPUS   I will not swear you, like some caitiff!
THESEUS   Nay,
    You would gain nothing more than my word gives you
ŒDIPUS   How will you do it?
THESEUS   What fear you specially?
ŒDIPUS   There will come those—
THESEUS   These will take care for them!
ŒDIPUS   Mind how you leave me—
THESEUS   Teach not me my duty!
ŒDIPUS   Needs must, who fears.

THESEUS   My spirit is not afraid.
ŒDIPUS   You do not know the threats—
THESEUS   I know that none
 Shall drag you from this place in spite of me.
 As for their threatenings—many are the threats
 In anger spoken often, but in vain;
 For when the reason has come home again,
 The threats are vanished. And for them, I know,
 Though they take heart to talk portentously
 Of carrying you away, yet it may happen
 The sea between us will be found full wide,
 And hardly navigable. I bid you, rather,
 Be of good cheer, apart from my resolve,
 Since Phœbus sent you hither; and, at least,
 Even in my absence, I am well assured
 My name will guard you from all injury.   [*Exit.*

Chorus

I. 1.

 Stranger, thou art come to rest
 Where the pasturing folds are best
 Of this land of goodly steeds,
 In Colonus' glistening meads,
 Where the clear-voiced nightingale
 Oftenest in green valley-glades
 Loves to hide her and bewail;
 Under wine-dark ivy shades,
 Or the leafy ways, untrod,
 Pierced by sun or tempest never,
 Myriad-fruited, of a God;
 Where in Bacchanalian trim
 Dionysus ranges ever
 With the Nymphs who fostered him;

I. 2.

 And with bloom each morning there
 Sky-bedewed, in clusters fair
 Without ceasing flourishes
 The narcissus, from of old
 Crown of mighty Goddesses,

And the crocus, rayed with gold;
Nor do sleepless fountains fail,
Wandering down Cephissus'[10] streams;
But with moisture pure return,
Quickening day by day the plains
In the bosom of the vale;
These nor choirs of Muses spurn,
Nor the Queen with golden reins,
Aphrodita, light-esteems.

II. 1.

Also there is a plant, self-sown,
Untrained, ungrafted—never known,
That I have heard, in Asian soil,
Or Pelops' mighty Dorian isle,
Which, terror of the spears of foes,
In this our land most largely grows—
Grey nurse of boyhood, the Olive-Leaf;
Plant neither youth nor veteran chief
Shall e'er destroy with violent hand;
For that the face of Jove above it,
An ever watching guardian, and
The azure-eyed Athana, love it.

II. 2.

And further, more than all, we boast
The great God's bounty, prized the most
Of honours by our Mother-state—
Fair sea, fleet steed, and fruitful strain.
O Cronos' son, Poseidon, King,
Thou givest her this praise to sing!
Thou didst for these highways create
The bit, the courser to refrain;
And thy good oar-blades, fashioned meet
For hands of rowers, with bounding motion
Follow the Nereids' hundred feet,
In marvellous dance, along the Ocean.

---

[10]*Cephissus*] The largest river in the region of Attica, where Athens was the principal city.

ANTIGONE   O highest extolled of lands, it is for thee
      To illustrate, now, these glorious words of praise.
ŒDIPUS   What is there new, my daughter?
ANTIGONE   Here comes Creon
      To meet us, father, and not escort-less.
ŒDIPUS   Now let the bourn of safety stand revealed,
      Friendliest of seniors, on your part, for me!
1 CITIZEN   Courage, it is at hand. If we are old,
      The vigour of our country has not aged.

                [*Enter* CREON, *attended.*]

CREON   Gentle inhabitants of this your land,
      I read it in your eyes, you have conceived
      Some sudden apprehension at my coming;
      But spare reproach, and have no fear of me.
      For with no forceful aim am I come hither,
      Being an old man, and knowing I am arrived
      Before a city of no meaner power
      Than any in Hellas;[11] rather, I am sent—
      Old as I am—for to persuade this man
      To come along with me to Theban soil,
      Not upon one man's errand, but enjoined
      By all the folk, since it has fallen to me,
      By kinship, to bewail most grievously
      Of our whole city his calamities.
      Now therefore, O thou luckless Œdipus,
      Listen to me, and turn thy footsteps home.
      All the whole Cadmean people call for thee,
      And rightly; and among them I the most;
      Who, if I be not basest of mankind,
      As much the most, old sir, grieve at thy troubles,
      Beholding thee in misery, far from home,
      And yet a wanderer always, tramping on,
      Indigent, leaning on one handmaiden,
      Who I—God help me! never had surmised
      Could fall to such a depth of ignominy
      As this unhappy one has fallen to,
      Thee and thy blindness tending evermore
      In habit of a beggar—at her age—
      Maiden as yet, but any passer's prey!

[11]*Hellas*] Greece.

What, is it shocking, the reproach I cast
On you, and on myself, (wretch that I am!)
And the whole house? Then by our fathers' Gods,
Since what is blazed abroad can not stay hidden,
Hearken to me, and hide it, Œdipus;
Consent to seek your city and father's roof;
Not without salutation to this town,
For she deserves it well; yet it were just
More worship should be paid to her at home,
Who was your foster-mother formerly.

ŒDIPUS   Thou aweless villain, ready to adduce
Specious invention of just argument
From every case, why this attempt on me?
Why do you seek to take me, a second time,
In such a snare as must torment me most
If I were in your power? For formerly,
When I was sick of my domestic ills,
When to avoid the land had charms for me,
You would not grant the favour I desired;
But when I was now sated of my frenzy,
And it was pleasant to wag on at home,
Straightway you thrust me forth! you cast me out!
Never a jot you cared for all this kinship!
And now once more, when you perceive this city
And all her sons in friendship at my side,
You try, with your soft cruel words, to part us!
And yet what charm lies in befriending men
Against their will? since if a man to you
Refused a favour, when you begged for it,
And would give nothing, and then afterwards,
When you were satisfied of your desire,
And all the grace was graceless, proffered it,
Would not the pleasure so received be vain?
Such are the offers which you make to me,
Good in pretence, but evil in the trial.
Yea, these shall hear how I will prove you base;
You are come to take me, yet not take me home,
But plant me in your confines, that your city
May come off free from harm, of this land's doing:
You shall not have it! This, though, you shall have;
My spirit for evil haunting evermore
About your land; and this my sons shall have,
As much of my domain as may suffice

   For them to die in! Can I not discern
   Better than you what is the case of Thebes?
   Far better; having better oracles,
   Phœbus, and Zeus himself, who is his sire.
   But treacherous is the tongue you have brought hither,
   And of sharp edges; and in using it
   You shall take more to hurt you, than to heal.
   But—for I know I make no way with you—
   Go! and let us live here. Give us content,
   We are well enough provided, as we are.
CREON Do you think my game is lost, as to your matters,
   In this discussion, rather—or your own?
ŒDIPUS All that I care for is that you should fail
   Either to persuade me, or these by-standers.
CREON O wretched man, have you no growth of sense,
   At last, to boast of? Do you hug reproach
   To your old age?
ŒDIPUS   You are adroit in tongue;
   But righteous know I none, who speaks fair speeches
   Whate'er his cause.
CREON   To say what's seasonable,
   And to say much, are different.
ŒDIPUS   You, no question,
   Say—O how little—and that seasonable!
CREON Not in the judgment of a mind like yours!
ŒDIPUS Depart; for I will speak for these as well;
   Do not come cruising, keeping watch on me,
   Where I must dwell.
CREON   These I attest, not you;
   But for the answer you will make your friends,
   If I once catch you—
ŒDIPUS   Who can capture me
   Against the will of my defenders?
CREON   Yea,
   Capture apart, you will be vexed anon.
ŒDIPUS What sort of act is there behind this menace?
CREON Of your two daughters one I have just seized
   And sent; and her I will take presently.
ŒDIPUS O sorrow!
CREON You will have more occasion to sing sorrow,
   Immediately, for this!
ŒDIPUS   You have seized my daughter?
CREON [*pointing to* ANTIGONE] Yes, and will seize her, soon!

ŒDIPUS   Ho, gentlemen!
     What will you do? Will you prove false to me?
     Will you not hunt the villain off your soil?
1 CITIZEN   Withdraw sir, straightway; for you deal not rightly
     In this; nor yet in what you did before.
CREON   [to the attendants] Now is your time; carry the girl away;
     By force, if she will not consent to go.
ANTIGONE   Unhappy, whither shall I fly? What help
     Of God or man shall I lay hold on?
1 CITIZEN   Sir,
     What are you doing?
CREON   I will not touch the man;
     Only this maiden, who belongs to me.
ŒDIPUS   You lords of Athens!
1 CITIZEN   Sir, you do not rightly!
CREON   I do.
1 CITIZEN   How rightly?
CREON   I carry off what is mine.

                                              [Seizes ANTIGONE.

ŒDIPUS   Help, Athens!

Chorus

          What d'ye mean, sirrah stranger?
          Will you not leave hold?
          You will come, presently,
          To a trial of force!

CREON   Keep off!

Chorus

          Not from you, till you desist.

CREON   I tell you, you will have to fight my city,
     If you do me a harm.
ŒDIPUS   Did I not say so?
1 CITIZEN   [to the attendant] Take your hands off that maiden
          instantly!
CREON   Keep your commands for those you rule!
1 CITIZEN   I tell you,
     Let go!
CREON   [to the attendants] And I tell you, to go your ways.

Chorus

Come on, here, come!
Come on, neighbours all!
The town is being spoiled—
Our town, by force of arms!
Come on, here, to me!

ANTIGONE   I am dragged away, unhappy! O sirs—sirs!
ŒDIPUS   Where are you, daughter?
ANTIGONE   Here, borne along perforce.
ŒDIPUS   Reach out your hands, my child!
ANTIGONE   I am not able.
CREON   Will you not take her on?

[Exeunt attendants with ANTIGONE.

ŒDIPUS   Wretch that I am!
CREON   At least you shall not any longer make
    Of these two crutches an excuse to roam;
    But since you choose to gain a victory
    At the expense of your own land, and friends,
    By whose commands, although myself am royal,
    I do these things, why take it! for in time
    You will find out, I know, that neither now
    Are you doing well to your own self, nor yet
    Did so before, crossing your friends, to indulge
    The frenzy, which is your perpetual bane.
1 CITIZEN   Hold there, sir stranger!
CREON   Touch me not, I say.
1 CITIZEN   If they are lost, I will hold fast to you!
CREON   You shall soon spare a weightier pledge to Thebes;
    For I will lay my hands not on them only.
1 CITIZEN   What will you turn to?
CREON   I will seize him too,
    And carry him off!
1 CITIZEN   You speak a perilous word.
CREON   I swear it shall be done forthwith.
1 CITIZEN   Unless
    The ruler of this country hinder you!
ŒDIPUS   O shameless voice! Would'st thou lay hands on me?
CREON   Silence, I say!
ŒDIPUS   Nay, may these Goddesses
    Leave me but breath enough to lay this curse
    On thee, thou monster! who hast torn away

No other than an eye—by force—from me,
Lost—like the eyes I lost before! For this,
May the all-seeing among Gods, the Sun,
Give to thyself, and to thy family,
Even such a life in thy old age as mine!

CREON   You natives of this country, mark you this?
ŒDIPUS   They mark us both, and understand that I,
Wronged by thy deeds, with words defend myself.
CREON   I will not check my fury; though alone,
And slow with age, I will arrest him here.
ŒDIPUS   Unhappy that I am!

Chorus

> How swollen is the pride
> You are come with hither,
> If you think, sir stranger,
> To accomplish this!

CREON   I think it.

Chorus

> Not, so long as Athens stands!

CREON   In his own right a weak man overcomes
A strong one.
ŒDIPUS   Hear ye what he mutters?
1 CITIZEN   What
He never will perform, (Zeus be my witness!)
CREON   That Zeus may know; you cannot.
1 CITIZEN   Is not this
Violence?
CREON   Yea, violence! but ye must bear it!

[*Attacks* ŒDIPUS.

Chorus

> Help, people all!
> Help, lords of the land!
> Come on quickly, come!
> They pass here, indeed,
> Beyond all the bounds!

[*Enter* THESEUS, *attended.*]

THESEUS   What cry was that? What is it? In what panic fear
    Did you stay me sacrificing at the altar here
    To the Sea-God your patron? Speak, tell me the need
    At which I have hurried hither, with less ease than speed.
ŒDIPUS   O dearest friend—for your accost I know—
    I have but now been miserably abused
    At this man's hands!
THESEUS   How? Who misused you? Speak!
ŒDIPUS   Creon here, whom you see, has torn away
    The one poor pair of children left to me!
THESEUS   How say you?
ŒDIPUS   You have heard how I am wronged.
THESEUS   Some servant go as quick as possible
    To the altars by, and make the people all—
    Horsemen and footmen—from the sacrifice
    Hurry, with loosened reins, to the chief points
    Where pathways meet by which the packmen come,
    Lest the girls pass, and I become a mock
    To this my guest, worsted by violence.
    Go, as I bid you, quickly;   [*Exit Guard.*
            As for him,
    Were I as far in anger as he merits,
    I had not suffered him to pass unscathed
    Out of my hands; but now, with the same law
    Shall he be suited, which he brought with him—
    That, and no other—Sir! you shall not stir
    Out of this country more, till you have brought
    And set those maidens here, for all to see;
    Since you have wrought unworthily of me,
    And of your lineage, and of your own land,
    Who, entering on a state that cares for right,
    And decides nothing without precedent,
    Must set at nought our country's officers,
    And in this onslaught hale away by force
    And make a prize of anything you please;
    Deeming my city to be void of men,
    Or manned with slaves, and my own self worth nothing!
    And yet it was not Thebes taught you this baseness;
    Thebes is not used to nourish lawless men,
    Nor would approve you, if she heard of you
    Despoiling me, yea and the Gods, by force

Dragging away poor creatures—suppliants.
I, if I did intrude upon your land,
Even if I had a cause more just than any,
Never, without the country's ruler's leave,
Whoever he might be, should have been found
Haling and leading captive; but I know
How guest to host ought to comport himself.
But you disgrace a state, that deserved better—
Your own—by your own act; and your full years
Leave you at once devoid of sense, and old.
So said I once before, and I now tell you;
Except you want to be compelled to stay
Against your will, an alien, in this land,
Have the girls brought back hither instantly!
You hear me say it, and what I say, I mean.

1 CITIZEN   Do you see the pass you have arrived at, Sir?
How you seem honest by your parentage,
And are found doing deeds iniquitous?

CREON   Not for that I account this city void
Of counsel or of manhood, as thou sayest,
O son of Ægeus, have I done this thing;
But apprehending no enthusiasm
About my kindred could have fallen on these,
That they, against my will, should cherish them;
And I felt certain they would not receive
A man polluted, and a parricide,
Nor one with whom was found the consciousness
Of an incestuous wedlock; such a Hill
Of Ares, rich in counsel, I well knew
To be established in this land of theirs,
That suffers not such vagabonds to dwell
Within their city's bounds; and in that trust
I undertook to make this capture mine.
And even this I should not have essayed,
But for the bitter curse by him denounced
On me, and on my race; for which, being wronged,
This, in return, I judged it right to do.
For of resentment there is no old age,
Other than death. No fret can reach the dead.
Now, you will do just what you please; for me—
Me friendlessness makes insignificant,
Although my words are just; yet when assailed,
Old as I am, I will attempt revenge.

ŒDIPUS   O front of impudence! Which thinkest thou
           Now to defile—My grey hairs, or thine own?
           Who hast spit forth out of thy mouth at me
           Murders and marriages and accidents,
           Which to my grief, not of free will, I suffered;
           Such was the will of Heaven, that had some cause
           For wrath, it may be, with our house, of old.
           Since for myself, I know you cannot find
           Any reproach of wrongfulness in me,
           That could have doomed me to commit these wrongs
           Against myself and mine; for, answer me,
           If to my father by an oracle
           The revelation came that he should die
           By his son's hands, how can you justly tax
           Me with the fact, whom neither father yet
           Then had begot, or mother had conceived,
           Me, who as yet had not begun to be?
           And if thereafter proving—as I proved—
           Hapless, I did lay hands upon my sire
           And slay him, nowise knowing what I did,
           Nor yet to whom I did it, how, I ask,
           Can you with reason blame the unconscious deed!
           And for my mother—are you not ashamed,
           O miserable! at forcing me to name
           Her marriage, your own sister's—as I will—
           I will not now be silent, you being grown
           To such a monster of outspokenness!
           She bare—ah yes, unknowingly she bare
           Me—who not knew! Woe worth the while to me!
           And having given me birth, she brought me forth
           Children—her own reproach! But of set purpose,
           For one thing, well I know, you spit this venom
           On her, and me; whereas I wedded her
           Unwitting, and unwillingly speak of it.
           But not for this my marriage, nor for that—
           That parricide, which you continually
           Throw in my teeth, bitterly upbraiding it,
           Do I consent to be called infamous.
           For answer me a question; but this one;
           If any person here upon the spot
           Drew near to kill you—you the just one—whether
           Would you enquire if he that sought your life
           Were your own father, or requite him straight?

You would requite the offender, I conceive,
If you love life; not look about for law.
Just such was the misfortune I incurred,
Led by the hand of Heaven; for which, I fancy,
Not even my father's spirit, were he alive,
Could say one word against me. And yet you—
(For just you are not, but think well to utter
All things, both lawful and unlawful,) you
Slander me with these sayings before them all!
Yea, you make free to fawn on Theseus' name,
And upon Athens—how decorously
She hath been ordered; and so lauding her,
You miss out this, that if there be a land
That knows what reverence to the Gods is due,
'Tis she herein excels, whence to remove
Me, the old suppliant, you assail my person,
And seize my daughters, and make off with them.
Wherefore these maiden Powers I invoke
With supplications, and with prayers adjure
To come, as aiders and auxiliaries;
So you may learn what sort of men they are,
By whom this city is defended.

1 CITIZEN   Sir,
The stranger is a good man; and his woes
Are horrible, and worthy of relief.

THESEUS   Enough of words; they speed, who have done the wrong,
While we, of the injured party, stand here still.

CREON   What is it you bid a poor weak man to do?

THESEUS   To shew the way, and to take me along,
That, if you have these maidens, whom we seek,
Inside our bounds, yourself may find them for me;
But if your guards are making off with them,
We need not toil; for there are others there,
No laggards, whom they never shall evade,
Crossing our frontiers, to give thanks to Heaven.
Lead forward! Know, sir captor, you are caught!
Fortune has trapped you, hunter! So it is,
Nothing abides of what is got by guile.
And you shall have no help; I am sure you have come
Not single, nor unfurnished, to the point
Of violence, such as you have here essayed,
But there was some one whom you trusted in.
I must look to it; I must not let this city

Be feebler than a single mortal's arm.
Do you take my sense? Or does my speaking seem
As idle, now, as when you framed this project?
CREON   Being here, you may say on, I shall not cavil;
But once at home, I shall know my part, too.
THESEUS   Ay, threaten us, and so—march! You, Œdipus,
Abide securely here; and credit me,
Till I have given your children to your arms,
Except I shall die first, I will not leave it.
ŒDIPUS   God speed you, Theseus, for your nobleness,
And for your duteous providence towards me.

[*Exeunt* THESEUS, CREON *and Guards.*

Chorus

I. 1.

I wish that I could be
Where foes are gathering fast,
Soon to be hurled together, brand on brand,
With clamour of battle! along either strand—
Pythian, or that where by the torches' light
Sit Queens, dispensing many a holy rite
To worshipping mortals on whose lips hath passed,
In mystic ritual, the golden key
Borne by their ministering Eumolpidæ;[12]
Soon, methinks, there
Shall Theseus, the awakener of the fight,
And that unconquered virgin pair,
Amid the fields hard by,
Join voices in one loud effectual rescue-cry!

I. 2.

Or haply pass they now
Out from the Œatid meads,
Nigh to that snow-clad mountain's western brow,
Flying on fleet steeds
Or swift contending chariots? He shall fail!
The battle spirit of our Athenian race
Is terrible; terrible in pride of place

[12]*Eumolpidæ*] Priests.

Are Theseus' children; lo where brightly shines
Curb beyond curb, and all along the lines
Of bridle-piece on bridle-piece of mail
    Come charging on
Horsemen on horses, warriors who revere
Athana, her to whom the horse is dear,
And him, the Sea-God, the land's guardian, Rhea's own son![13]

II. 1.

  Are they at work? Do they linger yet?
    How I court the thought I shall greet, ere long,
Those maids much injured—the maids who met
    From kindred hands injurious wrong.
Zeus works—he is working a thing to-day;
    Prophet am I of a well-won field;
O would that I were as a storm-winged dove,
Swift and sure, on a cloud above
To soar to Heaven, and so survey
    The arms that triumph, the arms that yield!

II. 2.

Hail, great Master of Gods in heaven,
    All-seeing Zeus! With conquering might
To the chiefs of our land by Thee be it given
    To obtain this prize—to achieve this fight!
So Pallas Athana, thy awful maid,
    Grant it! Phœbus, too, I invoke,
The Hunter-God—come, visit us here,
With the chaser of dappled swift-footed deer,[14]
Thy sister—come, bring aid upon aid
    To this our country and these our folk!

1 CITIZEN   You will not say, sir wanderer, to your seer,
    He is no sayer of sooth; for I perceive
    Those girls conducted hither back again.
ŒDIPUS   Where? where? How say you?—What was that you said?

---

[13]*Rhea*] Titan, wife of Cronus, mother of Poseidon, Hera, Pluto, Ceres, and Hestia.
[14]The reference is to Artemis, goddess of the hunt and Apollo's sister.

[*Enter* THESEUS, ANTIGONE, ISMENE *and Guards.*]

ANTIGONE   O father, father, might some Deity
    Give you to look upon this best of men,
    Who brings us back to you!
ŒDIPUS   Child, are you there,
    You and your sister?
ANTIGONE   Yes; for Theseus' hands
    And his good followers', here, redeemed us.
ŒDIPUS   Come,
    My girl—Come to your father, both of you,
    And let me clasp your form—as I despaired
    Ever should be!
ANTIGONE   Have what you ask—the leave,
    Not without longing.
ŒDIPUS   Where—where are you?
ANTIGONE   Here,
    Both of us, coming close.
ŒDIPUS   My darling sprays!
ANTIGONE   O ay, dear to the stem!
ŒDIPUS   Props of my frame!
ANTIGONE   Poor hapless props, of a poor frame indeed!
ŒDIPUS   I have my darlings! Now I could even die
    Not all unhappy, these being by my side.
    Daughters, support me—one on either hand—
    Growing to the plant, from which you took your growth,
    So shall you end this wretched groping—lonely
    Until you came; then tell me, in fewest words,
    All that has happened; tender maids like you
    Need not to make long speeches.
ANTIGONE   Father dear,
    This is the man who rescued us; to him
    You must give ear; his is the deed; my part
    Will be full brief.
ŒDIPUS   O Sir, be not amazed,
    If seeing my children here, out of all hope,
    Makes me prolong discourse to weariness.
    For well I know, this kindness, joy to me,
    No other than yourself has shewn towards them.
    For you, and no man else, delivered them;
    And may the Gods bestow as I desire
    On you, and on this land; since among you
    Alone of men did I find piety,

And gentle dealing, and all truthfulness.
I know it, and these thanks are my return;
For what I have, I have, only through you.
And now, O king, stretch out your hand to me,
For me to touch, and kiss, if kiss I may,
That forehead. Yet—what am I babbling! How
Can I desire that you should touch a man—
Wretch that I am! to whom what taint of ills
Cleaves not? I cannot; nor will suffer you;
Only the man who has experienced it
Can sympathize with misery such as mine.
There, where you stand, I greet you; and henceforth
Be duly mindful of me, as to-day.

THESEUS   That in the pleasure these your children bring
You set wide bounds to your discourse of it,
That you preferred their converse in my room,
I have not felt amazement; no annoy
Possesses me, for this; I do not care
To have my life made glorious with fine speeches,
Rather than by my actions. And I shew it;
Seeing I have failed in nought of what I sware,
Old man, to you; for here they are with me,
Alive, unharmed of what was threatened them.
And now, what need to make a bootless boast
Of how the field was won? things which yourself
Will come to know from these, having them with you;
But on a matter I have met withal
In coming here just now, advise with me;
Since, though it seems a trifle, it is strange;
And it behoves us to make light of nothing.

ŒDIPUS   What is it, son of Ægeus? Tell me; I
Know nothing of the things you hint.

THESEUS   They say
A man, who is no countryman of yours,
And yet akin, has come and seated him
Before our altar of Poseidon here,
Where I was offering, when you summoned me.

ŒDIPUS   What countryman? What is it that he seeks
In taking sanctuary?

THESEUS   I do not know;
Save only that with you, as I am told,
He asks for a few words, an easy boon.

ŒDIPUS   But of what kind? This is no sanctuary
Taken for a trifling matter.

THESEUS   As they say,
  The object of his journey is to come
  To speech of you; then to depart, in safety,
  The way he came.
ŒDIPUS   Who can it be, that seats him
  As suppliant thus?
THESEUS   Think if you have some kinsman
  In Argos, who might seek this boon of you.
ŒDIPUS   O best of friends, stop, say no more!
THESEUS   What ails you?
ŒDIPUS   Do not request me—
THESEUS   To what purport, say?
ŒDIPUS   I know full well who is the suppliant,
  When I hear this.
THESEUS   Who can it be, with whom
  I am to have a quarrel?
ŒDIPUS   O king, my son;
  My abhorred son, whose words of all men's else
  Most grievously could I endure to hear.
THESEUS   But why? Can you not listen, and still not do
  What you mislike? How is the hearing pain?
ŒDIPUS   Most alien to a father's ears, sir king,
  Has that voice grown; do not put stress on me
  To yield in this.
THESEUS   Look if the sanctuary
  Does not compel it; whether a regard
  Must not be paid towards the God.
ANTIGONE   My father,
  Hearken to me, young though I am who speak.
  Suffer this friend to gratify the God
  And his own heart, in that which he desires;
  And grant it us, to let our brother come.
  Take heart! You cannot be seduced, perforce,
  From your resolve, by words that grate on you;
  But where's the harm of hearing? By discourse
  Are deeds, maliciously designed, bewrayed.
  You gave him being; then, if he did to you
  The wickedest and worst of injuries,
  Not even so, dear father, were it right
  For you to do him evil in return.
  O let him come! Others have bad sons too,
  And keen resentments; but, on being advised,
  They are charmed in spirit by the spells of friends.

Look to the past, not to the present; all
That you endured through mother and through sire;
If you regard it, you will find, I know,
That harmful passion ends in further harm.
You have reminders of it far from slight,
Maimed of your sightless eyes. Let us prevail!
It is not right that they whose prayers are just
Should play the beggar; nor that you yourself,
Who are being kindly treated, should not know
How to requite the kindness you receive.

ŒDIPUS   Child, I am conquered, by your words and his;
Your pleasure is my pain; be it as you please;
Only, if he you speak of shall come hither—
Sir host—never let any one get power
Over my life!

THESEUS   Twice to be told such things
I do not need; once is enough, old man;
Nor would I boast; yet be sure, safe you are,
If any of the Gods takes care of me.

[*Exit* THESEUS, *attended.*

Chorus

I.

Whoso thinks average years a paltry thing,
        Choosing prolonged old age,
He, to my mind, will be found treasuring
        A foolish heritage.
For when a man hath given him to fulfil
        What length of days he will,
Then many things are dealt him, in long days,
        That border hard on pain,
And things that please are hidden from the gaze;
        And when the doom of Hades is made plain,
Whereto belongs no bridal, and no quire,
        Nor any sound of lyre,
                Death, at the end,
        Waits, an impartial friend.

II.

Never to have been born is much the best;
        And the next best, by far,

To return thence, by the way speediest,
　　Where our beginnings are.
While Youth is here, with folly in his train,
　　(So full of cares our lot,)
Whose feet can fare beyond the reach of pain?
　　What pains beset them not?
Murders, seditions, battles, envy, strife;
　　Yea and old age, in hateful friendlessness,
This is our portion at the close of life,
　　　　Strengthless—companionless;
　　　　　　Wherewith abide
　　　Ills passing all beside.

Such are the aged; such am I;
　　But he, this man of woes,
Is beaten down on every hand,
　　Like to some wintry Northern strand,
　　Vext by the Ocean's blows;
Such waves of ill, so fell and high,
　　Smite him, without repose;
Some from the settings of the Day,
　　Some from his rising light,
Some on the midmost noontide ray,
　　Some from the Alps of Night.

ANTIGONE　And here we have the stranger, I suppose—
　　Nay, father, unattended—coming up
　　This way; his eyes are wet with streaming tears.
ŒDIPUS　Who is the man?
ANTIGONE　　　　　　　The same whom all along
　　We guessed at, Polynices. He is here.

[*Enter* POLYNICES.]

POLYNICES　Alack, what shall I do, girls? Must I first
　　Mourn my own ills, or this my aged sire's,
　　Beholding him? Whom I have met withal
　　Outcast with you, here, on a foreign soil,
　　Clad in a garb, whose horrid grime antique
　　Has grown to suit with his antiquity,
　　Marring his frame, while on the breeze his hair
　　Streams from his eye-abated front uncombed,
　　And, as it seems, akin to these, he bears

The scrip, for his poor belly's provender!
The which I recreant all too late perceive,
And do confess I am proved the worst of men
By your condition. Ask what I have done
Of none but me. But seeing how Clemency,
Even by the side of Zeus, sharing his throne,
Rules, in all acts, so let her find a place,
Father, with you; for remedies, indeed,
Still may remain, of what has been amiss,
But aggravations none. — Why are you silent?
Father, say something! Do not turn away!
Will you return me not an answer back?
Insult me with a dumb dismissal? Tell
Not even why you are enraged with me?
O offspring of this man, sisters of mine,
Try you to move our father's countenance,
Inexorable, unapproachable,
Not to dismiss me, the God's worshipper,
Thus in disgrace, answering me never a word!

ANTIGONE   Unhappy brother, what you come to seek
Tell us yourself; for out of many words,
Stirring delight, or breathing pity, or pain,
Come, to the voiceless, powers of utterance.

POLYNICES   I will speak out; for you direct me well;
First calling to my aid the God himself,
Up from whose shrine the sovereign of this land
Raised me, and sent me hither, promising me
Audience and answer and safe conduct hence.
The which I shall expect to meet with, sirs,
From you, from these my sisters, and my sire.
Next, I would tell you, father, why I came.
I have been driven out of my native land,
Because I claimed, being of an elder birth,
To seat me upon your imperial throne;
For which Eteocles, though my junior born,
Not overthrowing me in argument,
Nor coming to the test of arms or act,
But tampering with the people, exiled me.
Whereof the cause, above all else, I say,
Is your Erinys; and from soothsayers,
Moreover, so I hear. For when I came
To Argos of the Dorians, I obtained
The daughter of Adrastus to my wife,

And made confederates along with me
As many of the land of Apia
As are deemed first, and have been best approved
In war; meaning to gather against Thebes
My host of the Seven Lances in their train,
And either die upon the field, or else
Banish the authors of my banishment.
So be it! Then, why am I come hither now?
Father, with expiatory prayers to you,
Both for myself and my allies, who now
In seven arrays under seven pennons stand
All round the plain of Thebes. Among them comes
Amphiaraus the strong spearman, first
In war, first in the acts of augury;
The second is Ætolian, Œneus' son,
Tydeus; a third Eteoclus, Argive-born;
Talaus his father sends Hippomedon
Fourth; and the fifth, Capaneus, vaunts himself
That he will set the castle of Thebes on fire
And burn it to the ground; the sixth springs forward,
Parthenopæus the Arcadian, named
As being born of mother theretofore
Long time untamed, the trusty progeny
Of Atalanta; and your own son I—
(Or if disowned, then by ill destiny
Begotten, but at least called yours), I lead
The undaunted host of Argos against Thebes.
And all together for these children's sake,
Father, beseech you, and by your own life,
Praying you relax your heavy wrath at me,
Now marching to avenge me of that brother
Who thrust me forth, spoiled of my father-land.
For if there is a truth in oracles,
They say success is to the side you choose.
Wherefore I implore you, by the water-springs—
Yea by the Gods of Thebes, hearken and yield;
For I am poor and exiled; so are you;
And under the same lot both you and I
Cringe to a stranger for a lodging. He
Meanwhile, at home, a monarch, well a day!
Lives delicately, and derides us both;
But with short effort, after small delay,
If you cooperate with my design,

Him will I shatter! and so take you home,
And in your own house place you, and myself,
And cast him out by force. With your goodwill
I may indulge this boast; but, without you,
I must lack strength even to come off with life.
1 CITIZEN   Now for his sake who sent him, Œdipus,
    Say what is meet, and send the man away.
ŒDIPUS   Sirs, wardens of this country—were not he
    Theseus, who sped him on his way to me,
    Deeming it fitting I should answer him,
    He never should have heard my voice at all!
    But now, being so far graced, he shall depart
    With that within his ears shall sober him
    All his life long. O most desertless villain,
    Who, when you held the sceptre and the throne
    Which now your brother has achieved in Thebes,
    Yourself expelled me—your own father—me
    Made homeless—drove to wear this livery,
    Which you shed tears to see, now you have come
    To walk in the same evil straits with me!
    This is no stuff to weep for; rather is it
    For me to bear, mindful, howe'er I live,
    That you are my destroyer. For you made me
    Familiar with this woe; you exiled me;
    And by your act made vagabond, I beg
    My daily bread from others. Had I not
    Fathered these girls, to be my cherishers,
    I had been dead, for aught you did for me;
    But now these keep me, these my cherishers,
    These men, not women, for their ministering;
    And ye are sprung from others' loins, not mine,
    Wherefore Heaven frowns upon thee—yea, not yet
    As it soon shall frown, if these cohorts move
    Toward Theba's hold; for it may never be
    That thou shalt storm that city; rather, first,
    Thou, and thy brother as well, blood-stained, shalt fall.
    Such curses upon you I denounced before,
    And summon, now, to come and fight for me,
    And make you learn true filial reverence,
    And cease your scorn, although the sire be blind,
    Who fathered sons like you! These did not so.
    Therefore thy supplication and thy throne
    Fall 'neath its sway, if Justice as of old

Sits equal in the ancient rule of Jove.
Hence! I disown thee, reptile! of base souls
Basest! and take with thee this doom of mine,
Never to win thy native land in fight,
Nor to return to Argos in the Vale,
But by a kindred hand thyself to fall,
Him having slain, who was thy banisher.
This is my curse! And to the abyss I call,
Hated, of Hades, where my father is,
To be thy place of exile; and I call
These Powers, and Ares, who in both of you
Hath sown this monstrous hate. Hear me, and go;
And as you go, tell all the Cadmeans,
Ay, and your trusty allies, what recompense
Is to his own sons dealt, by Œdipus.

1 CITIZEN I am sorry, Polynices, for the errand
On which you came; now get you back with speed.

POLYNICES   Woe for my journey, woe for my mischance,
Woe for my comrades! To an end like this
Did we set out from Argos on our way!
Such as it is impossible to tell
To any of my fellows, or to turn
Their footsteps backward; only this is left,
Silent, to meet my fate. O misery!
Sisters of mine, his daughters! You have heard
The hard words of our father, cursing me;
I charge you in Heaven's name, if that father's curse
Shall be fulfilled, and a return for you
Be granted home, do not you look on me
With contumely, but lay me in my tomb,
And grant me funeral rites. Then on that praise
Which from your labour for your father's sake
You now derive, shall rise a second praise,
As ample, through your ministering to me.

ANTIGONE   Polynices, I entreat you, yield to me!

POLYNICES   Tell me in what, dearest Antigone!

ANTIGONE   March back at once to Argos! Do not ruin
Yourself—and Thebes!

POLYNICES   That is impossible;
How could I lead the selfsame army forth,
If I had faltered once?

ANTIGONE   But why again
Must you get angry, boy? Where is your profit

In overthrowing your country?

POLYNICES   . To be banished
    Is a dishonour; and for me, the elder,
    To be so flouted by my brother.
ANTIGONE   Then
    Do you not see that you are carrying out
    His prophecies forthright, who spells you death,
    Each from the other's hand?
POLYNICES   He wishes it.
    No, no retreat is left us.
ANTIGONE   Woe for me!
    But who that heard the things he prophesied
    Will dare to follow?
POLYNICES   Nay, we will tell no tales.
    It is the merit of a general
    To impart good news, and to conceal the bad.
ANTIGONE   Is this the course you have resolved on, boy?
POLYNICES   Ay—stay me not. Now to this course of mine
    Must I give heed, luckless and evil made
    By him, my father, and his cleaving curse.
    But as for you, God speed you, as you do
    My hest in death—since you will have nought further
    To do for me in life. Unhand me now.
    Farewell. You will behold my face no more.
ANTIGONE   O woe is me!
POLYNICES   Do not lament for me.
ANTIGONE   Who but must mourn thee, brother, rushing thus
    On death foreseen?
POLYNICES   If needs must, die I will.
ANTIGONE   Not so, but hear me!
POLYNICES   Ask not what may not be.
ANTIGONE   Unhappy that I am, if I lose thee!
POLYNICES   This is in Destiny's hands, or thus to be,
    Or not to be. For you—the Gods I pray
    You never meet with ill; for you deserve,
    All will confess, not to be miserable.   [*Exit.*

Chorus

I. 1.

    Here are new griefs, new and calamitous,
    From sources new, made manifest to us,

Of the blind stranger's making;
Except, indeed, his fate is overtaking:
For of no doom from Heaven can I declare 'tis vain.
The end Time sees, yea, sees alway;
Time, that o'erthrows to-day,
Time, that with morning's light uprears again.   [*Thunder.*

1 CITIZEN   Heavens! how it thundered!
ŒDIPUS   Children, my children! will some bystander
Fetch the most excellent Theseus hither?
ANTIGONE   Father,
What is the end for which you summon him?
ŒDIPUS   This thunder, winged by Jove, must carry me
Straightway to Hades. Send at once, I say.   [*Thunder.*

Chorus

I. 2.

Hark with what might the unutterable roar
Of Jove's own bolt comes crashing down once more!
The very hair on my head
Stands up for dread;
My spirit quails.—There flames lightning from Heaven again!
What will the issue be?
I tremble at it: for surely not in vain
Is it sent forth—never innocuously.

[*Loud thunder.*

1 CITIZEN   You mighty Heavens! Thou Jove!
ŒDIPUS   Daughter, the appointed ending of my life
Has found me, and may not be averted more.
ANTIGONE   How do you know it? By what conjecture comes
This certainty?
ŒDIPUS   I feel it. With all speed
Let some one go and fetch this country's king.   [*Thunder.*

Chorus

II. 1.

Hark again, hark,
The echoing clap resounds on either hand.

Have mercy, O God, have mercy, if aught of dark
   Thou art now bringing to our mother-land!
      May he bring luck who meets me!
      Nor, now the man who greets me
   Is fraught with doom, let it be mine to share
   A fruitless boon—King, Jove, to thee I make my prayer!

ŒDIPUS   Is the man nigh, my children? Will he come
      While I still live, and reason rules my mind?
ANTIGONE   What is the trust, which in your mind you crave
      To breathe in Theseus' ears?
ŒDIPUS   To pay to him,
      For good he did me, a complete return,
      Such as I promised in receiving it.

Chorus

II. 2.

   Hither, my son,
      Quick, quick—howbeit thine offerings are placed
   High in the hollow of his altar-stone
      To the sea's lord, Poseidon, come with haste!
         Thee and thy city and friends
         The stranger-guest pretends
      To pay with profit, for his profiting,
   In righteous measure. Hasten and come forth, our king!

[*Enter* THESEUS, *attended.*]

THESEUS   What is this general din, sounding anew,
      Loud from yourselves, and from the stranger plain?
      Is it that bolt from Jove, or shower of hail,
      Has burst upon you? Anything, while Heaven
      Is raising such a storm, is credible.
ŒDIPUS   King, thou art here at need; yea, and some God
      Has given thee good speed of this thy way.
THESEUS   What is the new event which has arisen,
      O son of Laius?
ŒDIPUS   End of life to me.
      And I am anxious not to die forsworn,
      In what I promised to this city and thee.
THESEUS   But under what death-symptom do you labour?

ŒDIPUS   The Gods are their own heralds, telling me,
    Belying nought of tokens fixed before.
THESEUS   How do you say that this is shewn you, sir?
ŒDIPUS   The frequent thunderings continuous,
    And frequent-flashing arrows, from the hand
    Invincible—
THESEUS   You move me; for I see
    You are a mighty soothsayer, and your words
    Do not come false. Say, then, what we must do.
ŒDIPUS   I will inform thee, son of Ægeus,
    Of what shall be in store for this thy city,
    Beyond the harm of time. Of my own self,
    Without a hand to guide me, presently
    I will explore a spot wherein, in death,
    I am to rest. Never to any man
    Say where 'tis hidden, or whereabouts it lies;
    So may it ever bring thee vigour, more
    Than many bucklers, or the hireling spear
    Of neighbours. But the place—a mystery
    Not to be put in language, thou thyself
    Shalt learn when thou goest thither, but alone;
    For not to any of these citizens,
    Nor to my daughters, though I love them well,
    Will I declare it. Keep it to thyself;
    And, when thou art coming to the end of life,
    Disclose it but to one, thy foremost; he
    To him who shall come after shewing it,
    For ever. So shalt thou inhabit still
    This city, unwasted by the earth-sprung seed;
    While swarms of towns, however men may live
    Good neighbours, lightly try to injure you.
    For the Gods mark it well, though they are slow,
    When any turn to folly, and forsake
    Their service; such experience, Ægeus' son,
    Do thou eschew; nay, what I preach, thou knowest.
    Now—to the place! The message from on high
    Urges me forth; let us not linger now.
    Here, follow me, my daughters! in my turn,
    Look, I am acting as a guide to you,
    As you were mine, your father's. Come along!—
    Nay, do not touch me; let me for myself
    Search out the hallowed grave where, in this soil,
    It is my fate to lie. Here, this way, come;

This way! for Hermes the Conductor and
The Nether Queen are this way leading me.
O Light—my Dark—once thou wast mine to see;
And now not ever shall my limbs again
Feel thee! Already I creep upon my way
To hide my last of life in Hades. Thou,
Dearest of friends—thy land—thy followers—all,
May you live happy; and in your happiness
Fortunate ever, think of me, your dead!

[*Exeunt* ŒDIPUS, THESEUS, ANTIGONE, ISMENE, *and attendants.*

Chorus

1.

If sound of my prayers may rise unto Her who is hid from sight,
If worship of mine may approach thee, the King of the shadows of
                night,
                Aïdoneus, Aïdoneus[15]—
                I entreat that this stranger
May pass right well, without sound of grief, by a painless doom,
To the hiding-place of the dead beneath, and the Stygian home.
—Though many are the sorrows that visit thee, many thy labours in
                vain,
It may be, a Power that is righteous intends to uplift thee again.

2.

Hail, Queens of the realms of Earth! All hail, the unconquered frame
Of the Hound,[16] that crouched, we were told, at the Gate whither all
                men came,
                And growled from its caverns,
                (So the story went ever,)
As Hades' champion and guard—whose steps, I pray, may be led
Far off, when the stranger comes to the nether fields of the dead!
—O Thou that art born of Earth, the begotten of the Deep,
Thee I invoke, the giver of unending sleep.

[*Enter a Messenger.*]

---

[15]*Aïdoneus*] Pluto, God of the Infernal Regions.
[16]*the Hound*] Cerberus, the multi-headed dog which guards the gates to the
    Underworld.

MESSENGER   Sirs, to cut short, as far as possible,
          What I would say—Œdipus is no more;
          But for what there befell, there are no words
          To tell it in brief space; nor was it brief,
          All that was done.
1 CITIZEN   Is the poor wanderer gone?
MESSENGER   Yes, he is quit of his life-trouble.
1 CITIZEN   How?
          Was't by some heaven-sent end—poor soul—and calm?
MESSENGER   Truly the event is meet to wonder at.
          First, in what fashion he set forth from hence,
          You must have seen, being present, even as I;
          None of his company conducting him,
          But he himself shewing to us all the way.
          Next, having reached the threshold of that chasm
          Whose root is in the Brazen Stairs below,
          There, upon one of the diverging paths,
          Nigh to the hollowed basin where are kept
          The tokens of the sure-abiding bond
          'Twixt Perithous and Theseus, he stood still;[17]
          Thence halfway to the stone from Thoricus,[18]
          Betwixt the hollow pear-tree and marble tomb,
          He sate him down; then doffed his grimy robe;
          And then, crying to his daughters, bade them bring
          Waters to wash, and pour, out of some stream;
          Which twain, proceeding to the opposing slope
          Of verdurous Demeter, with small delay
          Brought to their father that he sent them for;
          And him they washed, and decked in such attire
          As is in use; and when, now, nought remained
          Unsatisfied of all that he desired,
          Sounded from Hades thunder, and the maids,
          As they heard, shivered; and at their father's knees
          Fell down, and wept, beating their breasts, and raised
          Wailings prolonged, unceasing. He the while,
          Soon as he heard their bitter note of woe,
          Folding his arms about them, said; "For you,
          My girls, this day there is no father more;

---

[17]Perithous and Theseus together attempted to rescue Persephone from Hades, but they
    were unable to outdo Pluto.
[18]Thoricus was another hero of the region. His stone, the pear tree and the marble
    tomb are all presumed to have been sacred spots, ritual stopping points on the route
    to Hades.

For all things now are ended that were mine;
And now no longer need you bear for me
The burden of your hard tendance, hard indeed—
I know it, my children; but one single word
Cancels the evil of all cares like this;
Love, which ye had from no one more than me;
Of whom bereft, you for the time to come
Must live your life." So they all wept aloud,
Clinging to each other; but when they were come
To end of lamentation, and the cry
Rose up no longer, silence reigned awhile.
Then suddenly some voice shouted his name;
So that the hair of all stood up for fear;
For a God called him—called him many times,
From many sides at once: "Ho, Œdipus,
Thou Œdipus, why are we tarrying?
It is full long that thou art stayed for; come!"
He, when he felt Heaven summoned him, bespake
That the land's king, Theseus, should come to him;
And, when he came, said to him, "O dear friend,
Pledge me, in the ancient fashion, your right hand
To these my children, (and you, girls, give him yours,)
And swear—never to yield them willingly,
But as you purpose now to accomplish all
In kindness, ever, that is good for them."
He, of his gentleness, agreed; and sware,
(But not condoling,) to his guest, to do it.
And straightway as he sware it, Œdipus,
Touching with sightless hands his daughters, said:
"Now, children, you must leave this place; bear up
In spirit, as befits your nobleness;
Look not upon the sights you may not see,
List not the voices which you must not hear,
But with all speed depart; let but the king,
Theseus, be present, and behold the end."
While he thus spake, we hearkened, all of us;
Then followed we the maidens, grieving sore,
With streaming tears. When we had gone apart,
After short space we turned, and saw far off—
The man, indeed, nowhere still visible—
Only the king's self, holding up his hand
Over his face, so as to shade his eyes,
As if some sight of terror had appeared,

Awful, intolerable to gaze upon;
Then, in a moment, without interval,
We saw him kneel, worshipping Earth, and Heaven
The abode of Gods, both in one act, together.
But he—what death he died, save Theseus' self
There lives not any mortal who can tell.
For neither any fire-fraught thunderbolt
Rapt him, from Heaven, nor whirlwind from the sea
Stirred up to meet the moment; but some guide
Sent from above, or depth of the earth beneath
Opening to take him, friendly, without pain.
For not as of one mourned, or with disease
Grown pitiable, was his departure; but
If any ever was so, wonderful.
—If what I say seems folly, I can spare
The assent of those to whom I seem a fool.

1 CITIZEN   And where now are his daughters, and those friends
Who did attend them?

MESSENGER   They, at least, not far;
For sounds of wailing unmistakeable
Declare them to be moving up this way.

[*Enter* ANTIGONE *and* ISMENE.]

I. 1.

ANTIGONE   Alas, it is for us, it is for us to rue,
Not once alone, but evermore anew,
Unhappy that we are, the fatal strains
Of our sire's blood implanted in our veins.
For whom, erewhile,
We ceaselessly endured a world of toil,
And have to tell, at last, of most unmeasured ill,
Beheld and suffered, still.

1 CITIZEN   But what has happened?

ANTIGONE   You can guess it, friends.

1 CITIZEN   He is gone?

ANTIGONE   Yes, as one would most wish for him
—What wonder? In whose way
Nor war nor ocean lay,
But viewless regions rapt him home,
Sudden, by some mysterious doom,

While on our sight
The gloom of night,
Deathful and desolate, is come.
For how shall we sustain
Life's heavy load of toil,
Wandering o'er the billowy main,
Or on some foreign soil?

ISMENE   I know not. O that with my sire's last breath
I by some sudden death
Might perish! for the life that is to be
Seems worse than death to me.

Chorus

O children, worthiest pair, what heaven may send
Bear—to the end,
And let your grief be mild; the way by which you came
You have no cause to blame.

I. 2.

ANTIGONE   Even the ills of life, it may be, we regret.
For what indeed was no-wise charmful, yet
Became, to me, a life not without charms
The while I had my father in my arms.
O father dear,
Wrapped evermore in nether darkness drear,
O not for thine old age mightest thou ever be
Unloved by her and me!

1 CITIZEN   He fared—?
ANTIGONE   He fared even as he wished to do.
1 CITIZEN   How was it?
ANTIGONE   Upon that foreign soil he chose
Died he! For ever laid
Low, in the kindly shade,
He left behind no tearless grief,
No measured mourning, dull and brief,
These eyes are wet
With weeping yet,
Nor know I how to find relief.
Oh not for thy desire
In a strange land to die,

Need'st thou have perished, O my sire,
　　　Thus, with no loved ones by!
ISMENE　　O wretched that I am! What future fate
　　　Me must await
And thee, my sister, lingering here alone,
　　　And our dear father gone!

Chorus

But now he is at last thus happily
　　　From life set free,
Cease this lamenting, friends! From evils, in some shape,
　　　No mortal can escape.

II. 1.

ANTIGONE　　Back let us haste, dear sister!
ISMENE　　　　　　　　　　　What to do?
ANTIGONE　　A longing is upon me—
ISMENE　　　　　　　　What?
ANTIGONE　　　　　　　　　　To view
　　　The earth-bound home—
ISMENE　　　　　　　Of whom?
ANTIGONE　　Our father—woe is me!
ISMENE　　But is it not forbid? Do you not see?
ANTIGONE　　Why should it make you chide?
ISMENE　　This too, that—
ANTIGONE　　　　　　Well, what next?
ISMENE　　　　　　　　　　Without a tomb,
　　　Lonely, he died!
ANTIGONE　　Take me to him, and slay me by his side!
ISMENE　　Alas, unhappy, whither should I flee,
　　　To live, once more, a life of misery,
　　　In the old loneliness and poverty!

II. 2.

1 CITIZEN　　Dear friends, fear nought!
ANTIGONE　　　　　　　　　　Where should I shelter me?
1 CITIZEN　　Truly there was a shelter, long ago—
ANTIGONE　　How?
1 CITIZEN　　　For your fortunes, that they should be free

From evil destiny.
ANTIGONE   Nay, that I know.
1 CITIZEN   What is it, then, that doubles your concern?
ANTIGONE   'Tis that I know no way for our return
          To our own home.
1 CITIZEN   Care not to seek it!
ANTIGONE   I am overcome
          With weariness.
1 CITIZEN   Time was, you were so.
ANTIGONE   Yea,
          Sorely before, but now surpassingly.
1 CITIZEN   Truly it was yours to stem a stormy sea!
ANTIGONE   Whither, O Jove, shall we direct our way?
          Towards what point of hope—alas the day!
          Doth God impel me, and forbid my stay?

III.

[*Enter* THESEUS, *attended.*]

THESEUS   Children, cease to lament; for griefs, where
          Grace from the Nether Gods awaits us,
          Blessing all fortunes,
             Sorrow is causeless; nay, were sin.
ANTIGONE   O son of Ægeus, we are thy suppliants.
THESEUS   For what boon, my children?
ANTIGONE   We too
          Fain would look on our father's tomb.
THESEUS   Nay, the approach to it is forbidden us.
ANTIGONE   King, how say you, master of Athens?
THESEUS   He, my children, gave me commandment
          That no mortal's foot should trespass
          Near those precincts,
          Or give name to the ark of refuge
          Where he dwells; which things, he told me,
          Duly observing,
          I might evermore keep these confines
          Free from annoyance;
          And so Heaven o'erheard me swear it,
             And the omniscient Oath of Jove.
ANTIGONE   Well, if such be the way he willed it,
          Let that fully suffice. Now send us

        Back to our ancient Thebes; it may be
        We may ward off ruin, impendent
        O'er our brethren.
THESEUS   I will do it at once, and all things
        Such as I purpose, for your service,
        And his pleasure, our dead, this moment
        Rapt far from us; I may not tire.

                        Chorus

        Cease, no longer upraise your wailing;
            All these promises shall not fail.

                                        [*Exeunt.*

Antigone

Antigone, written and first performed in the late 440s B.C., is among Sophocles' most often revived plays; its strong roles, and its conflict between individual morality (championed by a brave young woman) and the overbearing political needs of the state, have never lost their compelling interest through the generations.

Although the events of *Antigone* concern the family of Oedipus and follow those of *Oedipus Rex* in logical time, the latter play postdates *Antigone* by over ten years.

To avoid too much footnoting, here is a brief summary of the legendary events leading up to the action of the play. When Oedipus, ruler of the city-state of Thebes, learned that he had killed his father and married his mother, he blinded himself, and his wife Jocasta killed herself. (They had had four children, the sons Eteocles and Polynices and the daughters Antigone and Ismene.) Oedipus lived on in the palace, where, vexed by the disobedience of his sons, he placed a curse on them to the effect that they would destroy each other. Indeed, they quarreled over supremacy in the city. Agreeing to govern in alternate years, they drew lots and the first year fell to Eteocles. Polynices, suspecting his brother's intentions, fled to the city of Argos, where he became son-in-law of its ruler, Adrastus. They prepared an invasion of Thebes, in association with other heroes (the Seven Against Thebes), each of the seven attacking a different gate of the city. All the invaders perished; the two brothers killed each other. Now Creon, Jocasta's brother, taking over the reins of government, has forbidden the burial of the traitor Polynices. (This was a terrible punishment, striking at the most elemental Greek feelings concerning the proper treatment of the dead; hence Antigone's irresistible urge to cover the body at least symbolically, with a handful of earth.)

STANLEY APPELBAUM

Persons Represented

ANTIGONE,
ISMENE, } *daughters of Oedipus, late king of Thebes.*

CREON, *brother to Jocasta, late queen of Thebes, Captain-general of the army, and successor to the throne.*

A Sentinel.

HÆMON, *son to Creon, betrothed to Antigone.*

TIRESIAS, *a seer.*

A Messenger in attendance on Creon.

EURYDICE, *wife to Creon.*

The CHORUS *is composed of Senators of Thebes.*

Guards; Attendants; a Boy leading Tiresias.

Antigone

Scene, before the Royal Palace at Thebes. Time, early morning. Enter ANTIGONE *and* ISMENE.

ANTIGONE.   Ismene, dear in very sisterhood,
Do you perceive how Heaven upon us two
Means to fulfil, before we come to die,
Out of all ills that grow from Œdipus—
What not, indeed ? for there's no sorrow or harm,
No circumstance of scandal or of shame
I have not seen, among your griefs, and mine.
And now again, what is this word they say
Our Captain-general proclaimed but now
To the whole city ?   Did you hear and heed ?
Or are you blind, while pains of enemies
Are passing on your friends ?

ISMENE.   Antigone,
To me no tidings about friends are come,
Pleasant or grievous, ever since we two
Of our two brothers were bereft, who died
Both in one day, each by the other's hand.
And since the Argive host in this same night
Took itself hence, I have heard nothing else,
To make me happier, or more miserable.

ANTIGONE.   I knew as much; and for that reason made you
Go out of doors—to tell you privately.

ISMENE.   What is it ? I see you have some mystery.

ANTIGONE.   What ! has not Creon to the tomb preferred
        One of our brothers, and with contumely
        Withheld it from the other ? Eteocles
        Duly, they say, even as by law was due,
        He hid beneath the earth, rendering him honour
        Among the dead below ; but the dead body
        Of Polynices, miserably slain,
        They say it has been given out publicly
        None may bewail, none bury, all must leave
        Unwept, unsepulchred, a dainty prize
        For fowl that watch, gloating upon their prey !
        This is the matter he has had proclaimed—
        Excellent Creon ! for your heed, they say,
        And mine, I tell you—mine ! and he moves hither,
        Meaning to announce it plainly in the ears
        Of such as do not know it, and to declare
        It is no matter of small moment ; he
        Who does any of these things shall surely die ;
        The citizens shall stone him in the streets.
        So stands the case. Now you will quickly show
        If you are worthy of your birth or no.

ISMENE. But O rash heart, what good, if it be thus,
        Could I effect, helping or hindering ?

ANTIGONE.   Look, will you join me ? will you work with me ?

ISMENE. In what attempt ? What mean you ?

ANTIGONE. .   Help me lift
        The body up—

ISMENE.   What, would you bury him ?
        Against the proclamation ?

ANTIGONE.   My own brother
        And yours I will ! If you will not, I will ;
        I shall not prove disloyal.

ISMENE.   You are mad !
        When Creon has forbidden it ?

ANTIGONE.   From mine own
    He has no right to stay me.
ISMENE.   Alas, O sister,
    Think how our father perished ! self-convict—
    Abhorred—dishonoured—blind—his eyes put out
    By his own hand ! How she who was at once
    His wife and mother with a knotted noose
    Laid violent hands on her own life ! And how
    Our two unhappy brothers in one day
    Each on his own head by the other's hand
    Wrought common ruin ! We now left alone—
    Do but consider how most miserably
    We too shall perish, if despite of law
    We traverse the behest or power of kings.
    We must remember we are women born,
    Unapt to cope with men ; and, being ruled
    By mightier than ourselves, we have to hear
    These things—and worse. For my part, I will ask
    Pardon of those beneath, for what perforce
    I needs must do, but yield obedience
    To them that walk in power ; to exceed
    Is madness, and not wisdom.
ANTIGONE.   Then in future
    I will not bid you help me ; nor henceforth,
    Though you desire, shall you, with my good will,
    Share what I do. Be what seems right to you ;
    Him will I bury. Death, so met, were honour ;
    And for that capital crime of piety,
    Loving and loved, I will lie by his side.
    Far longer is there need I satisfy
    Those nether Powers, than powers on earth ; for there
    For ever must I lie. You, if you will,
    Hold up to scorn what is approved of Heaven !
ISMENE. I am not one to cover things with scorn ;

But I was born too feeble to contend
Against the state.

ANTIGONE.   Yes, you can put that forward ;
But I will go and heap a burial mound
Over my most dear brother.

ISMENE.   My poor sister,
How beyond measure do I fear for you !

ANTIGONE.   Do not spend fear on me. Shape your own course.

ISMENE.   At least announce it, then, to nobody,
But keep it close, as I will.

ANTIGONE.   Tell it, tell it !
You'll cross me worse, by far, if you keep silence—
Not publish it to all.

ISMENE.   Your heart beats hotly
For chilling work !

ANTIGONE.   I know that those approve
Whom I most need to please.

ISMENE.   If you could do it !
But you desire impossibilities.

ANTIGONE.   Well, when I find I have no power to stir,
I will cease trying.

ISMENE.   But things impossible
'Tis wrong to attempt at all.

ANTIGONE.   If you will say it,
I shall detest you soon ;   and you will justly
Incur the dead man's hatred.   Suffer me
And my unwisdom to endure the weight
Of what is threatened.   I shall meet with nothing
More grievous, at the worst, than death, with honour.

ISMENE.   Then go, if you will have it :   and take this with you,
You go on a fool's errand !   [*Exit* ANTIGONE.
                         Lover true
To your beloved, none the less, are you !   ·   [*Exit.*

Enter THEBAN SENATORS, *as Chorus*.

CHORUS.

I. 1.

Sunbeam bright ! Thou fairest ray
  That ever dawned on Theban eyes
    Over the portals seven !
O orb of aureate day,
  How glorious didst thou rise
    O'er Dirca's[1] streams, shining from heaven,
Him, the man[2] with shield of white
Who came from Argos in armour dight
Hurrying runagate o'er the plain,[3]
Jerking harder his bridle rein ;
Who by Polynices' quarrellous broil
Stirred up in arms to invade our soil
    With strident cries as an eagle flies
  Swooped down on the fields before him,
'Neath cover of eagle pinion white
As drifted snow, a buckler bright
    On many a breast, and a horsetail crest
From each helm floating o'er him.

I. 2.

Yawning with many a blood-stained spear
  Around our seven-gated town
    High o'er the roofs he stood ;
Then, or ever a torch could sear

---

[1] Spring and river at Thebes.
[2] Adrastus, one of the seven leaders of the invaders of Thebes.
[3] The orb is hurrying the man into retreat.

With flames the rampart-crown—
    Or ever his jaws were filled with blood
Of us and ours, lo, he was fled !
Such clatter of war behind him spread,
Stress too sore for his utmost might
Matched with the Dragon[1] in the fight ;
For Zeus abhors tongue-glorious boasts ;
And straightway as he beheld their hosts,
Where on they rolled, covered with gold,
    Streaming in mighty eddy,
Scornfully with a missile flame
He struck down Capaneus,[2] as he came
Uplifting high his victory-cry
    At the topmost goal already.

II. 1.

Tantalus-like[3] aloft he hung, then fell ;
    Earth at his fall resounded ;
Even as, maddened by the Bacchic spell,
    On with torch in hand he bounded,
      Breathing blasts of hate.
So the stroke was turned aside,
    Mighty Ares rudely dealing
Others elsewhere, far and wide,
    Like a right-hand courser wheeling
      Round the goals of fate.

For captains seven at portals seven
Found each his match in the combat even,
And left on the field both sword and shield

---

[1] The Thebans, descendants of men generated from dragon's teeth.
[2] Another of the Seven Against Thebes.
[3] Like Tantalus, tormented by hunger and thirst in the underworld.

As a trophy to Zeus, who o'erthrew them ;
Save the wretched twain, who against each other
Though born of one father, and one mother,
Laid lances at aim—to their own death came,
    And the common fate that slew them.

II. 2.

But now loud Victory returns at last
    On Theban chariots smiling,
Let us begin oblivion of the past,
    Memories of the late war beguiling
      Into slumber sound.
  Seek we every holy shrine ;
    There begin the night-long chorus ;
  Let the Theban Boy divine,
    Bacchus, lead the way before us,
      Shaking all the ground.

Leave we the song : the King is here ;
Creon, Menœceus' son, draws near ;
To the function strange—like the heaven-sent change
  Which has raised him newly to power :
What counsel urging—what ends of state,
That he summons us to deliberate,
The elders all, by his herald's call,
  At a strange unwonted hour ?

Enter CREON, *attended.*

CREON.   Sirs, for the ship of state—the Gods once more,
       After much rocking on a stormy surge,
       Set her on even keel. Now therefore you,
       You of all others, by my summoners
       I bade come hither ; having found you first
       Right loyal ever to the kingly power

In Laius' time ; and next, while Œdipus
Ordered the commonwealth ; and since his fall,
With steadfast purposes abiding still,
Circling their progeny. Now, since they perished,
Both on one day, slain by a two-edged fate,
Striking and stricken, sullied with a stain
Of mutual fratricide, I, as you know,
In right of kinship nearest to the dead,
Possess the throne and take the supreme power.
Howbeit it is impossible to know
The spirit of any man, purpose or will,
Before it be displayed by exercise
In government and laws. To me, I say,
Now as of old, that pilot of the state
Who sets no hand to the best policy,
But remains tongue-tied through some terror, seems
Vilest of men. Him too, who sets a friend
Before his native land, I prize at nothing.
God, who seest all things always, witness it !
If I perceive, where safety should have been,
Mischief advancing toward my citizens,
I will not sit in silence ; nor account
As friend to me the country's enemy ;
But thus I deem : she is our ark of safety ;
And friends are made then only, when, embarked
Upon her deck, we ride the seas upright.
Such are the laws by which I mean to further
This city's welfare ; and akin to these
I have given orders to the citizens
Touching the sons of Œdipus. Eteocles,
Who in this city's quarrel fought and fell,
The foremost of our champions in the fray,
They should entomb with the full sanctity
Of rites that solemnize the downward road

Of their dead greatest.   Him the while, his brother,
That Polynices who, returning home
A banished man, sought to lay waste with fire
His household Gods, his native country—sought
To glut himself with his own kindred's blood,
Or carry them away to slavery,
It has been promulgated to the city
No man shall bury, none should wail for him ;
Unsepulchred, shamed in the eyes of men,
His body shall be left to be devoured
By dogs and fowls of the air.   Such is my will.
Never with me shall wicked men usurp
The honours of the righteous ;   but whoe'er
Is friendly to this city shall, by me,
Living or dead, be honoured equally.

1 SENATOR.   Creon Menœceus' son, we hear your pleasure
Both on this city's friend, and on her foe ;
It is your sovereignty's prerogative
To pass with absolute freedom on the dead,
And us, who have survived them.

CREON.   Please to see
What has been said performed.

1 SENATOR.   That charge confer
On some one who is younger.

CREON.   Of the body ?
Sentries are set, already.

1 SENATOR.   Then what else
Is there, besides, which you would lay on us ?

CREON.   Not to connive at disobedience.

1 SENATOR.   There's no such fool as to embrace his death.

CREON.   Death is the penalty.   But men right often
Are brought to ruin, through their dreams of gain.

Enter a Sentinel.

SENTINEL.   My lord, I will not say—" breathless with speed
              I come, plying a nimble foot ; "   for truly
              I had a many sticking-points of thought,
              Wheeling about to march upon my rear.
              For my heart whispered me all sorts of counsel ;
              " Poor wretch, why go, to meet thy sentence ? "—
              " Wretch,
              Tarrying again ?   If Creon hear the news
              From others' lips, how shalt thou then not rue it ? "
              Out of this whirligig it came to pass
              I hastened—at my leisure ;   a short road,
              Thus, becomes long.   Nevertheless at last
              It won the day to come hither, to your presence ;
              And speak I will, though nothing have to say ;
              For I come clinging to the hope that I
              Can suffer nothing—save my destiny.

CREON.   Well—and what caused you this disheartenment ?

SENTINEL.   First let me tell you what concerns myself.
              I do protest, I neither did the deed,
              Nor saw it done, whoever 'twas who did it ;
              Nor should I rightly come to any harm.

CREON.   At all events you are a good tactician,
              And fence the matter off all round.   But clearly
              You have some strange thing to tell ?

SENTINEL.   Yes.   Serious tidings
              Induce much hesitation.

CREON.   Once for all
              Please to speak out, and make an end, and go.

SENTINEL.   Why, I am telling you.   That body some one
              Has just now buried—sprinkled thirsty dust
              Over the form—added the proper rites,
              And has gone off.

CREON.   What say you ?   What man dared
              To do it ?

SENTINEL.   I know not.   There was no dint there
        Of any mattock, not a sod was turned ;
        Merely hard ground and bare, without a break,
        Without a rut from wheels ;   it was some workman
        Who left no mark.   When the first day-sentry
        Shewed what had happened, we were all dismayed.
        The body had vanished ;   not indeed interred,
        But a light dust lay on it, as if poured out
        By one who shunned the curse ;   and there appeared
        No trace that a wild beast, or any hound,
        Had come, or torn the carcase.   Angry words
        Were bandied up and down, guard blaming guard,
        And blows had like to end it, none being by
        To hinder ;   for each one of us in turn
        Stood culprit, none convicted, but the plea
        " I know not " passed.   Ready were we to take
        Hot iron in hand, or pass through fire, and call
        The Gods to witness, that we neither did it,
        Nor were accessory to any man
        Who compassed it, or did it.   So at last,
        When all our searching proved to be in vain,
        There speaks up one, who made us, every man,
        Hang down our heads for fear, knowing no way
        To say him nay, or without scathe comply.
        His burden was, this business must be carried
        To you, without reserve.   That voice prevailed ;
        And me, poor wretch, the lot condemns to get
        This piece of luck.   I come a post unwilling,
        I well believe it, to unwilling ears ;
        None love the messenger who brings bad news.

1 SENATOR.   My lord, my heart misgave me from the first
        This must be something more than natural.

CREON.   Truce to your speech, before I choke with rage,
        Lest you be found at once grey-beard and fool !

To say that guardian deities would care
For this dead body, is intolerable.
Could they, by way of supereminent honour
Paid to a benefactor, give him burial,
Who came to fire their land, their pillared fanes
And sacred treasures, and set laws at nought ?
Or do you see Gods honouring the bad ?
'Tis false.   These orders from the first some people
Hardly accepted, murmuring at me,
Shaking their heads in secret, stiffening
Uneasy necks against this yoke of mine.
They have suborned these sentinels to do it,
I know that well.   No such ill currency
Ever appeared, as money to mankind :
This is it that sacks cities, this routs out
Men from their homes, and trains and turns astray
The minds of honest mortals, setting them
Upon base actions ;   this made plain to men
Habits of all misdoing, and cognizance
Of every work of wickedness.   Howbeit
Such hireling perpetrators, in the end,
Have wrought so far, that they shall pay for it.
So surely as I live to worship Jove,
Know this for truth ;   I swear it in your ears ;
Except you find and bring before my face
The real actor in this funeral,
Death, by itself, shall not suffice for you,
Before, hung up alive, you have revealed
The secret of this outrage ;   that henceforth
You may seek plunder—not without respect
Of where your profit lies ;   and may be taught
It is not good to covet all men's pay ;
For mark you !   by corruption few men thrive,
And many come to mischief.

SENTINEL.   Have I leave
    To say a word, or shall I turn and go ?
CREON.   Cannot you see your prating tortures me ?
SENTINEL.   Pricks you how deep ?   In the ears, or to the spleen ?
CREON.   Why do you gauge my chafing, where it lies ?
SENTINEL.   Your heart-ache were the doer's, your ear-ache mine.
CREON.   Out, what a bare-faced babbler born art thou!
SENTINEL.   Never the actor in this business, though!
CREON.   Yes, and for money you would sell your soul!
SENTINEL.   Plague on it! 'tis hard, a man should be suspicious,
    And with a false suspicion !
CREON.   Yes, suspicion ;
    Mince it as best you may. Make me to know
    Whose are these doings, or you shall soon allow
    Left-handed gains work their own punishment.   [*Exit.*
SENTINEL.   I wish he may be found. Chance must decide,
    Whether or no, you will not, certainly,
    See me returning hither. Heaven be praised
    I am in safety, past all thought or dream!   [*Exit.*

CHORUS

I. 1.

    Much is there passing strange ;
      Nothing surpassing mankind.
    He it is loves to range
    Over the ocean hoar,
    Thorough the surges' roar,
      South winds raging behind ;

    Earth, too, wears he away,
      The Mother of Gods on high,
    Tireless, free from decay ;
    With team he furrows the ground,

And the ploughs go round and round,
As year on year goes by.

I. 2.

The bird-tribes, light of mind,
    The races of beasts of prey,
And sea-fish after their kind,
Man, abounding in wiles,
Entangles in his toils
    And carries captive away.

The roamers over the hill,
    The field-inhabiting deer,
By craft he conquers, at will ;
He bends beneath his yoke
The neck of the steed unbroke,
    And pride of the upland steer.

II. 1.

He has gotten him speech, and fancy breeze-betost,
    And for the state instinct of order meet ;
He has found him shelter from the chilling frost
    Of a clear sky, and from the arrowy sleet ;
Illimitable in cunning, cunning-less
    He meets no change of fortune that can come ;
He has found escape from pain and helplessness ;
    Only he knows no refuge from the tomb.

II. 2.

Now bends he to the good, now to the ill,
    With craft of art, subtle past reach of sight ;

Wresting his country's laws to his own will,
   Spurning the sanctions of celestial right ;
High in the city, he is made city-less,
   Whoso is corrupt, for his impiety ;
He that will work the works of wickedness,
   Let him not house, let him not hold, with me !

At this monstrous vision I stand in
Doubt! How dare I say, well knowing her,
That this maid is not—Antigone !
     Daughter of Œdipus !
Hapless child, of a hapless father !
Sure—ah surely they did not find thee
Madly defying our king's commandments,
   And so prisoner bring thee here ?

Enter Sentinel with ANTIGONE.

SENTINEL.   This is the woman who has done the deed.
     We took her burying him. Where's Creon ?
1 SENATOR.   Here
     Comes he again, out of the house, at need.

Enter CREON.

CREON. What is it ? In what fit season come I forth ?
SENTINEL.   My lord, I see a man should never vow
     He will not do a thing, for second thoughts
     Bely the purpose. Truly I could have sworn
     It would be long indeed ere I came hither
     Under that hail of threats you rained on me.
     But since an unforeseen happy surprise
     Passes all other pleasing out of measure,
     I come, though I forswore it mightily,
     Bringing this maiden, who was caught in act
     To set that bier in order. Here, my lord,

No lot was cast ;   this windfall is to me,
And to no other. Take her, now, yourself ;
Examine and convict her, as you please ;
I wash my hands of it, and ought, of right,
To be clean quit of the scrape, for good and all.

CREON.   You seized—and bring—her ! In what way, and whence ?

SENTINEL.   Burying that man, herself ! You know the whole.

CREON.   Are you in earnest ?   Do you understand
What you are saying ?

SENTINEL.   Yes, that I saw this girl
Burying that body you forbade to bury.
Do I speak clear and plain ?

CREON.   How might this be,
That she was seen, and taken in the act ?

SENTINEL.   Why thus it happened. When we reached the place,
Wrought on by those dread menacings from you,
We swept away all dust that covered up
The body, and laid the clammy limbs quite bare,
And windward from the summit of the hill,
Out of the tainted air that spread from him,
We sat us down, each, as it might be, rousing
His neighbour with a clamour of abuse,
Wakening him up, whenever any one
Seemed to be slack in watching. This went on,
Till in mid air the luminous orb of day
Stood, and the heat grew sultry. Suddenly
A violent eddy lifted from the ground
A hurricane, a trouble of the sky ;
Ruffling all foliage of the woodland plain
It filled the horizon ;   the vast atmosphere
Thickened to meet it ;   we, closing our eyes,
Endured the Heaven-sent plague. After a while,
When it had ceased, there stands this maiden in sight,
And wails aloud, shrill as the bitter note

Of the sad bird, when as she finds the couch
Of her void nest robbed of her young ; so she,
Soon as she sees the body stripped and bare,
Bursts out in shrieks, and calls down curses dire
On their heads who had done it. Straightway then
She gathers handfuls of dry dust, and brings them,
And from a shapely brazen cruse held high
She crowns the body with drink-offerings,
Once, twice, and thrice. We at the sight rushed forward,
And trapped her, nothing daunted, on the spot ;
And taxed her with the past offence, and this
The present. Not one whit did she deny ;
A pleasant though a pitiful sight to me ;
For nothing's sweeter than to have got off
In person ; but to bring into mischance
Our friends is pitiful. And yet to pay
No more than this is cheap, to save one's life.

CREON. Do you, I say—you, with your downcast brow—
        Own or deny that you have done this deed ?
ANTIGONE.   I say I did it ; I deny it not.
CREON. Take yourself hence, whither you will, sir knave;
        You are acquitted of a heavy charge.   [*Exit Sentinel.*
        Now tell me, not at length, but in brief space,
        Knew you the order not to do it ?
ANTIGONE.   Yes,
        I knew it ; what should hinder ? It was plain.
CREON. And you made free to overstep my law ?
ANTIGONE.   Because it was not Zeus who ordered it,
        Nor Justice, dweller with the Nether Gods,
        Gave such a law to men ; nor did I deem
        Your ordinance of so much binding force,
        As that a mortal man could overbear
        The unchangeable unwritten code of Heaven ;
        This is not of today and yesterday,

But lives for ever, having origin
Whence no man knows : whose sanctions I were loath
In Heaven's sight to provoke, fearing the will
Of any man. I knew that I should die—
How otherwise ? even although your voice
Had never so prescribed. And that I die
Before my hour is due, that I count gain.
For one who lives in many ills, as I—
How should he fail to gain by dying ? Thus
To me the pain is light, to meet this fate ;
But had I borne to leave the body of him
My mother bare unburied, then, indeed,
I might feel pain ; but as it is, I cannot ;
And if my present action seems to you
Foolish—'tis like I am found guilty of folly
At a fool's mouth !

1 SENATOR. Lo you, the spirit stout
Of her stout father's child—unapt to bend
Beneath misfortune !

CREON. But be well assured,
Tempers too stubborn are the first to fail ;
The hardest iron from the furnace, forged
To stiffness, you may see most frequently
Shivered and broken ; and the chafing steeds
I have known governed with a slender curb.
It is unseemly that a household drudge
Should be misproud ; but she was conversant
With outrage, ever since she passed the bounds
Laid down by law ; then hard upon that deed
Comes this, the second outrage, to exult
And triumph in her deed. Truly if here
She wield such powers uncensured, she is man,
I woman! Be she of my sister born,
Or nearer to myself than the whole band

Of our domestic tutelary Jove,
She, and the sister—for her equally .
I charge with compassing this funeral—
Shall not escape a most tremendous doom.
And call her ; for within the house but now
I saw her, frenzied and beside herself ;
And it is common for the moody sprite
Of plotters in the dark to no good end
To have been caught, planning its knavery,
Before the deed is acted. None the less
I hate it, when one taken in misdoing
Straight seeks to gloss the facts !

ANTIGONE.   Would you aught more
Than take my life, whom you did catch ?

CREON.   Not I ;
Take that, take all.

ANTIGONE.   Then why do you delay ?
Since naught is pleasing of your words to me,
Or, as I trust, can ever please, so mine
Must needs be unacceptable to you.
And yet from whence could I have gathered praise
More worthily, than from depositing
My own brother in a tomb ? These, all of them,
Would utter one approval, did not fear
Seal up their lips. 'Tis tyranny's privilege,
And not the least—power to declare and do
What it is minded.

CREON.   You, of all this people,
Are singular in your discernment.

ANTIGONE.   Nay,
They too discern ; they but refrain their tongues
At your behest.

CREON.   And you are not ashamed
That you deem otherwise ?

ANTIGONE.   It is no shame
        To pay respect to our own flesh and blood.
CREON.   And his dead foeman, was not he your brother
        As well ?
ANTIGONE.   Yes, the same sire's and mother's son.
CREON.   Why pay, then, honours which are wrongs to him ?
ANTIGONE.   The dead clay makes no protest.
CREON.   Not although
        His with a villain's share your reverence ?
ANTIGONE.   It was no bondman perished, but a brother.
CREON.   Spoiling, I say, this country ;   while his rival
        Stood for it.
ANTIGONE.   All the same, these rites are due
        To the underworld.
CREON.   But not in equal measure
        Both for the good man and the bad.
ANTIGONE.   Who knows
        This is not piety there ?
CREON.   The enemy
        Can never be a friend, even in death.
ANTIGONE.   Well, I was made for fellowship in love,
        Not fellowship in hate.
CREON.   Then get you down
        Thither, and love, if you must love, the dead!
        No woman, while I live, shall order me.

CHORUS.

See where out by the doors Ismene
Weeping drops of sisterly grieving
Comes ;   and a cloud o'erhanging her eyebrows
Mars her dark-flushed cheek, and moistens
        Her fair face with pitiful tears.

Enter Attendants with ISMENE.

CREON.　And you—who like a viper unawares
　　　　Have crept into my house, and sucked me bloodless,
　　　　While I unknowingly was fostering you,
　　　　Twin furies, to the upsetting of my throne—
　　　　Come, tell me, will you say you also shared
　　　　This burying, or protest your innocence?

ISMENE.　Yes, I have done it—if Antigone
　　　　Says so—I join with her to share the blame.

ANTIGONE.　That justice will not suffer; you refused,
　　　　And I—I had no partner.

ISMENE.　　　　　　　　　　In your trouble
　　　　I do not blush to claim companionship
　　　　Of what you have to endure.

ANTIGONE.　　　　　　　　　　Whose was the deed
　　　　Death and the spirits of the dead can tell!
　　　　A friend in words is not a friend for me.

ISMENE.　Shame me not, sister, by denying me
　　　　A death, for honouring the dead, with you!

ANTIGONE.　Mix not your death with mine. Do not claim work
　　　　You did not touch. I shall suffice to die.

ISMENE.　And what care I for life, if I lost you?

ANTIGONE.　Ask Creon; you are dutiful to him.

ISMENE.　Why do you cross me so, to no good purpose?

ANTIGONE.　Nay, I am sick at heart, if I do make
　　　　My mock of you.

ISMENE.　　　　　　　Nay but what can I do,
　　　　Now, even yet, to help you?

ANTIGONE.　　　　　　　　　　Save yourself;
　　　　I do not grudge you your escape.

ISMENE.　　　　　　　　　　　O me
　　　　Unhappy! And must I miss to share your fate?

ANTIGONE.　You made your choice, to live; I mine, to die.

ISMENE.　Not if you count my words unsaid.

ANTIGONE.　　　　　　　　　　　By some

Your judgment is approved ; by others mine.

ISMENE. Then our delinquency is equal, too.

ANTIGONE. Take courage, you are living ; but my life
Long since has died, so I might serve the dead.

CREON. Of these two girls I swear the one even now
Has been proved witless ; the other was so born.

ISMENE. Ah sir, the wretched cannot keep the wit
That they were born with, but it flits away.

CREON. Yours did so, when you chose to join ill-doers
In their misdoing.

ISMENE.   How could I live on
Alone, without my sister ?

CREON.   Do not say
"My sister"; for you have no sister more.

ISMENE. What, will you put to death your own son's bride ?

CREON. He may go further afield—

ISMENE.   Not as by troth
Plighted to her by him.

CREON.   Unworthy wives
For sons of mine I hate.

ANTIGONE.   O dearest Hæmon,
How are you slighted by your father !

CREON.   I
Am weary of your marriage, and of you.

ISMENE. Your own son! will you tear her from his arms ?

CREON. Death will prevent that bridal-rite, for me.

1 SENATOR.   I see, the sentence of this maiden's death
Has been determined.

CREON.   Then we see the same.
An end of trifling. Slaves, there, take them in !
As women, henceforth, must they live—not suffered
To gad abroad ; for even bold men flinch,
When they view Death hard by the verge of Life.

                              [*Exeunt* ANTIGONE *and* ISMENE, *guarded*.

CHORUS.

I. 1.

Happy the man whose cup of life is free
    From taste of evil ! If Heaven's influence shake them,
   No ill but follows, till it overtake them,
All generations of his family ;
      Like as when before the sweep
        Of the sea-borne Thracian blast
        The surge of ocean coursing past
      Above the cavern of the deep
      Rolls up from the region under
        All the blackness of the shore,
      And the beaten beaches thunder
        Answer to the roar.

I. 2.

Woes upon woes on Labdacus' race[1] I see—
    Living or dead—inveterately descend ;
    And son with sire entangled, without end,
And by some God smitten without remedy ;
      For a light of late had spread
        O'er the last surviving root
      In the house of Œdipus ;
      Now, the sickle murderous
      Of the Rulers of the dead,
      And wild words beyond control,
      And the frenzy of her own soul,
        Again mow down the shoot.

[1] Labdacus was a descendant of the founder of Thebes, and an ancestor of Oedipus.

II. 1.

Thy power, O God, what pride of man constraineth,
Which neither sleep, that all things else enchaineth,
   Nor even the tireless moons of Heaven destroy ?
      Thy throne is founded fast,
High on Olympus, in great brilliancy,
      Far beyond Time's annoy.
Through present and through future and through
      past
   Abideth one decree ;
      Nought in excess
Enters the life of man without unhappiness.

II. 2.

For wandering Hope to many among mankind
Seems pleasurable ; but to many a mind
   Proves but a mockery of its wild desires.
      They know not aught, nor fear,
Till their feet feel the pathway strewn with fires.
      "If evil good appear,
That soul to his ruin is divinely led"—
      (Wisely the word was said !)
      And short the hour
He spends unscathed by the avenging power.

        Hæmon comes, thy last surviving
        Child. Is he here to bewail, indignant,
        His lost bride, Antigone ? Grieves he
          For a vain promise—her marriage-bed ?

Enter HÆMON.

CREON. We shall know soon, better than seers can tell us.
Son, you are here in anger, are you not,
Against your sire, hearing his final doom
Upon your bride to be ?   Or are we friends,
Always, with you, whate'er our policy ?

HÆMON.   Yours am I, father ; and you guide my steps
With your good counsels, which for my part I
Will follow closely ;   for there is no marriage
Shall occupy a larger place with me
Than your direction, in the path of honour.

CREON. So is it right, my son, to be disposed—
In everything to back your father's quarrel.
It is for this men pray to breed and rear
In their homes dutiful offspring—to requite
The foe with evil, and their father's friend
Honour, as did their father. Whoso gets
Children unserviceable—what else could he
Be said to breed, but troubles for himself,
And store of laughter for his enemies ?
Nay, never fling away your wits, my son,
Through liking for a woman ;   recollect,
Cold are embracings, where the wife is naught,
Who shares your board and bed. And what worse sore
Can plague us, than a loved one's worthlessness ?
Better to spurn this maiden as a foe !
Leave her to wed some bridegroom in the grave !
For, having caught her in the act, alone
Of the whole city disobeying me,
I will not publicly bely myself,
But kill her. Now let her go glorify
Her God of kindred ! If I choose to cherish
My own born kinsfolk in rebelliousness,
Then verily I must count on strangers too.
For he alone who is a man of worth

In his own household will appear upright
In the state also ;   and whoe'er offends
Against the laws by violence, or thinks
To give commands to rulers—I deny
Favour to such. Obedience is due
To the state's officer in small and great,
Just and unjust commandments ;   he who pays it
I should be confident would govern well,
And cheerfully be governed, and abide
A true and trusty comrade at my back,
Firm in the ranks amid the storm of war.
There lives no greater fiend than Anarchy ;
She ruins states, turns houses out of doors,
Breaks up in rout the embattled soldiery ;
While Discipline preserves the multitude
Of the ordered host alive. Therefore it is
We must assist the cause of order ;   this
Forbids concession to a feminine will ;
Better be outcast, if we must, of men,
Than have it said a woman worsted us.

1 SENATOR.   Unless old age have robbed me of myself,
I think the tenor of your words is wise.

HÆMON.   Father, the Gods plant reason in mankind,
Of all good gifts the highest ;   and to say
You speak not rightly in this, I lack the power ;
Nor do I crave it. Still, another's thought
Might be of service ;   and it is for me,
Being your son, to mark the words, the deeds,
And the complaints, of all. To a private man
Your frown is dreadful, who has things to say
That will offend you ;   but I secretly
Can gather this ;   how the folk mourn this maid,
" Who of all women most unmeriting,
For noblest acts dies by the worst of deaths,

Who her own brother battle-slain—unburied—
Would not allow to perish in the fangs
Of carrion hounds or any bird of prey ;
And " (so the whisper darkling passes round)
" Is she not worthy to be carved in gold ? "
Father, beside your welfare there is nothing
More prized by me ;   for what more glorious crown
Can be to children, than their father's honour ?
Or to a father, from his sons, than theirs ?
Do not persist, then, to retain at heart
One sole idea, that the thing is right
Which your mouth utters, and nought else beside.
For all men who believe themselves alone
Wise, or that they possess a soul or speech
Such as none other, turn them inside out,
They are found empty ;   and though a man be wise,
It is no shame for him to live and learn,
And not to stretch a course too far. You see
How all the trees on winter torrent banks,
Yielding, preserve their sprays ;   those that would stem it
Break, roots and all ;   the shipman too, who keeps
The vessel's main-sheet taut, and will not slacken,
Goes cruising, in the end, keel uppermost :
Let thy wrath go !   Be willing to relent !
For if some sense, even from a younger head,
Be mine to afford, I say it is far better
A man should be, for every accident,
Furnished with inbred skill ;   but what of that ?
Since nature's bent will have it otherwise,
'Tis good to learn of those who counsel wisely.

1 SENATOR.   Sir, you might learn, when he speaks seasonably ;
And you, from him ;   for both have spoken well.

CREON.   Men that we are, must we be sent to school
To learn discretion of a boy like this ?

HÆMON.   None that's dishonest ;   and if I am young,
It is not well to have regard to years
Rather than services.

CREON.   Good service is it,
To pay respect to rebels ?

HÆMON.   To wrongdoers
I would not even ask for reverence.

CREON.   Was it not some such taint infected her ?

HÆMON.   So say not all this populace of Thebes.

CREON.   The city to prescribe me my decrees !

HÆMON.   Look, say you so, you are too young in this !

CREON.   Am I to rule this land after some will
Other than mine ?

HÆMON.   A city is no city
That is of one man only.

CREON.   Is not the city
Held to be his who rules it ?

HÆMON.   That were brave—
You, a sole monarch of an empty land !

CREON.   This fellow, it seems, fights on the woman's side.

HÆMON.   An you be woman !   My forethought is for you.

CREON.   O villain—traversing thy father's rights !

HÆMON.   Because I see you sinning against right.

CREON.   Sin I, to cause my sway to be held sacred ?

HÆMON.   You desecrate, by trampling on Heaven's honour.

CREON.   Foul spotted heart—a woman's follower !

HÆMON.   You will not find me serving what is vile.

CREON.   I say this talk of thine is all for her.

HÆMON.   And you, and me, and for the Gods beneath !

CREON.   Never shall she live on to marry thee !

HÆMON.   Die as she may, she shall not die alone.

CREON.   Art thou grown bold enough to threaten, too ?

HÆMON.   Where is the threat, to speak against vain counsel ?

CREON.   Vain boy, thyself shalt rue thy counselling.

HÆMON.   I had called you erring, were you not my sire.

CREON. Thou woman's bondman, do not spaniel me !

HÆMON. Do you expect to speak, and not be answered ?

CREON. Do I so ? By Olympus over us,
If thou revile me, and find fault with me,
Never believe but it shall cost thee dear !
Bring out the wretch, that in his sight, at once,
Here, with her bridegroom by her, she may die !

HÆMON. Not in my sight, at least—not by my side,
Believe it, shall she perish ! And for thee—
Storm at the friends who choose thy company !
My face thou never shalt behold again. [Exit.

1 SENATOR. The man is gone, my lord, headlong with rage ;
And wits so young, when galled, are full of danger.

CREON. Let be, let him imagine more, or do,
Than mortal may ; yet he shall not redeem
From sentence those two maidens.

1 SENATOR. Both of them ?
Is it your will to slay them both alike ?

CREON. That is well said ; not her who did not touch it.

1 SENATOR. And by what death mean you to kill the other ?

CREON. Into some waste untrodden of mankind
She shall be drawn, and, in some rock-hewn cave,
With only food enough provided her
For expiation, so that all the city
Escape the guilt of blood, buried alive.
There, if she ask him, Hades, the one God
Whom she regards, may grant her not to perish ;
Or there, at latest, she shall recognize
It is lost labour to revere the dead. [Exit.

CHORUS.

O Love, thou art victor in fight : thou mak'st all things afraid ;
Thou couchest thee softly at night on the cheeks of a maid ;
Thou passest the bounds of the sea, and the folds of the fields ;

To thee the immortal, to thee the ephemeral yields ;
Thou maddenest them that possess thee ;   thou turnest astray
The souls of the just, to oppress them, out of the way ;
Thou hast kindled amongst us pride, and the quarrel of kin ;
Thou art lord, by the eyes of a bride, and the love-light therein ;
Thou sittest assessor with Right ;   her kingdom is thine,
Who sports with invincible might, Aphrodita divine.

Enter ANTIGONE, *guarded*.

> I too, myself, am carried as I look
> Beyond the bounds of right ;
> Nor can I brook
> The springing fountain of my tears, to see
> My child, Antigone,
> Pass to the chamber of universal night.

I. 1.

ANTIGONE.   Behold me, people of my native land :
            I wend my latest way :
        I gaze upon the latest light of day
            That I shall ever see ;
        Death, who lays all to rest, is leading me
            To Acheron's[1] far strand
        Alive ;   to me no bridal hymns belong,
            For me no marriage song
        Has yet been sung ;   but Acheron instead
            Is it, whom I must wed.

CHORUS.   Nay but with praise and voicings of renown
          Thou partest for that prison-house of the dead ;
          Unsmitten by diseases that consume,
          By sword unvisited,

[1] River in the underworld.

Thou only of mortals freely shalt go down,
Alive, to the tomb.

I. 2.

ANTIGONE. I have heard tell the sorrowful end of her,[1]
                    That Phrygian sojourner
            On Sipylus' peak, offspring of Tantalus ;
                    How stony shoots upgrown
            Like ivy bands enclosed her in the stone ;
                    With snows continuous
            And ceaseless rain her body melts away ;
                    Streams from her tear-flown head
            Water her front ;   likest to hers the bed
                    My fate prepares today.

CHORUS.   She was of godlike nature, goddess-sprung,
            And we are mortals, and of human race ;
            And it were glorious odds
            For maiden slain, among
            The equals of the Gods
            In life—and then in death—to gain a place.

II. 1.

ANTIGONE.   They mock me. Gods of Thebes ! why scorn you me
                    Thus, to my face,
                    Alive, not death-stricken yet ?
            O city, and you the city's large-dowered race,
                    Ye streams from Dirca's source,
            Ye woods that shadow Theba's chariot-course,

---

[1] Niobe, from Phrygia in Asia Minor. Her children were killed by Apollo and Artemis after she had boasted of being a more prolific mother than theirs. In her sorrow she turned to stone on the mountain.

Listen and see,
 Let none of you forget,
How sacrificed, and for what laws offended,
By no tears friended,
 I to the prisoning mound
Of a strange grave am journeying under ground.
Ah me unhappy ! home is none for me ;
 Alike in life or death an exile must I be.

CHORUS. Thou to the farthest verge forth-faring,
 O my child, of daring,
 Against the lofty threshold of the laws
 Didst stumble and fall. The cause
 Is some ancestral load, which thou art bearing.

II. 2.

ANTIGONE. There didst thou touch upon my bitterest bale—
 A threefold tale—
 My father's piteous doom,
Doom of us all, scions of Labdacus.
 Woe for my mother's bed !
Woe for the ill-starred spouse, from her own womb
Untimely born !
 O what a father's house
Was that from whence I drew my life forlorn !
To whom, unwed,
 Accursed, lo I come
To sojourn as a stranger in their home !
And thou too, ruined, my brother, in a wife,
 Didst by thy death bring death upon thy sister's life !

CHORUS. To pay due reverence is a duty, too :
 And power—his power, whose empire is confest,
 May no wise be transgressed ;
 But thee thine own infatuate mood o'er-threw.

ANTIGONE.   Friendless, unwept, unwed,
                         I, sick at heart, am led
                              The way prepared for me ;
                                 Day's hallowed orb on high
                              I may no longer see ;
                         For me no tears are spent,
                         Nor any friends lament
                                 The death I die.

Enter CREON.

CREON.   Think you that any one, if help might be
         In wailing and lament before he died,
         Would ever make an end ? Away with her !
         Wall her up close in some deep catacomb,
         As I have said ; leave her alone, apart,
         To perish, if she will ; or if she live,
         To make her tomb her tenement. For us,
         We will be guiltless of this maiden's blood ;
         But here on earth she shall abide no more.
ANTIGONE.   Thou Grave, my bridal chamber ! dwelling-place
         Hollowed in earth, the everlasting prison
         Whither I bend my steps, to join the band
         Of kindred, whose more numerous host already
         Persephone hath counted with the dead ;
         Of whom I last and far most miserably
         Descend, before my term of life is full ;
         I come, cherishing this hope especially,
         To win approval in my father's sight,
         Approval too, my mother, in thine, and thine
         Dear brother ! for that with these hands I paid
         Unto you dead lavement and ordering
         And sepulchre-libations ; and that now,
         Polynices, in the tendance of thy body
         I meet with this reward. Yet to the wise
         It was no crime, that I did honour thee.

For never had I, even had I been
Mother of children, or if spouse of mine
Lay dead and mouldering, in the state's despite
Taken this task upon me. Do you ask
What argument I follow here of law ?
One husband dead, another might be mine ;
Sons by another, did I lose the first ;
But, sire and mother buried in the grave,
A brother is a branch that grows no more.
Yet I, preferring by this argument
To honour thee to the end, in Creon's sight
Appear in that I did so to offend,
And dare to do things heinous, O my brother !
And for this cause he hath bid lay hands on me,
And leads me, not as wives or brides are led,
Unblest with any marriage, any care
Of children ;   destitute of friends, forlorn,
Yet living, to the chambers of the dead
See me descend. Yet what celestial right
Did I transgress ?   How should I any more
Look up to heaven, in my adversity ?
Whom should I call to aid ?   Am I not come
Through piety to be held impious ?   If
This is approved in Heaven, why let me suffer,
And own that I have sinned ;   but if the sin
Belong to these—O may their punishment
Be measured by the wrongfulness of mine !

1 SENATOR.   Still the same storms possess her, with the same
Precipitance of spirit.

CREON.   Then for this
Her guards shall rue their slowness.

ANTIGONE.   Woe for me !
The word I hear comes hand in hand with death !

1 SENATOR.   I may not say Be comforted, for this
          Shall not be so ; I have no words of cheer.
ANTIGONE.   O City of Theba ! O my country ! Gods,
          The Fathers of my race ! I am led hence—
          I linger now no more. Behold me, lords,
          The last of your kings' house—what doom is mine,
          And at whose hands, and for what cause—that I
          Duly performed the dues of piety !

                              [*Exeunt* ANTIGONE *and guards.*

                         CHORUS.

                          I. 1.

          For a dungeon brazen-barred
            The body of Danae endured
              To exchange Heaven's daylight of old,
          In a tomb-like chamber immured,
          Hid beneath fetter and guard ;
          And she was born, we are told,
            O child, my child, unto honour,
            And a son[1] was begotten upon her
          To Zeus in a shower of gold.
          But the stress of a Fate is hard ;
          Nor wealth, nor warfare, nor ward,
            Nor black ships cleaving the sea
            Can resist her, or flee.

                          I. 2.

          And the Thracians' king, Dryas' son,[2]
            The hasty of wrath, was bound

          _____

          [1] The hero Perseus.
          [2] Lycurgus. In his madness he killed his wife and children.

For his words of mocking and pride ;
  Dionysus closing him round,
Pent in a prison of stone ;
Till, his madness casting aside
  Its flower and fury wild,
  He knew what God he reviled—
Whose power he had defied ;
Restraining the Mænad choir,[1]
Quenching the Evian[2] fire,
  Enraging the Muses' throng,
  The lovers of song.

II. 1.

And by the twofold main
  Of rocks Cyanean[3]—there
    Lies the Bosporean strand,
And the lone Thracian plain
  Of Salmydessus, where
    Is Ares' border-land :
Who saw the stab of pain
  Dealt on the Phineid pair[4]
    At that fierce dame's command ;
Blinding the orbits of their blasted sight,
Smitten, without spear to smite,
  By a spindle's point made bare,
  And by a bloody hand.

---

[1] Wild female devotees of Dionysus.

[2] Dionysus'.

[3] The clashing rocks at the entrance to the Black Sea; all the geographical terms here indicate this area.

[4] The sons of Phineus, a local seer, who blinded them at the urging of his second wife, their stepmother. Their mother was Kleopatra, a daughter of Boreas, the north wind, and of an Athenian woman (a daughter of King Erectheus) whom he had abducted.

II. 2.

They mourned their mother dead,
  Their hearts with anguish wrung,
    Wasting away, poor seed
Of her deserted bed ;
  Who, Boreas' daughter, sprung
    From the old Erechtheid breed,
In remote caverns fed
  Her native gales among,
    Went swiftly as the steed,
Offspring of Heaven, over the steep-down wild ;
Yet to her too, my child,
  The Destinies, that lead
    Lives of long ages, clung.

Enter TIRESIAS *led by a boy.*

TIRESIAS.   Princes of Thebes, two fellow-travellers.
    Debtors in common to the eyes of one,
    We stand before you ; for a blind man's path
    Hangs on the guide who marshals him the way.
CREON.   What would'st thou now, reverend Tiresias ?
TIRESIAS.   That will I tell. Do thou obey the seer.
CREON.   I never have departed hitherto
    From thy advice.
TIRESIAS.   And therefore 'tis, thou steerest
    The city's course straight forward.
CREON.   Thou hast done me
    Good service, I can witness.
TIRESIAS.   Now again
    Think, thou dost walk on fortune's razor-edge.
CREON.   What is it ? I tremble but to see thee speak.
TIRESIAS.   Listen to what my art foreshadoweth,
    And thou shalt know. I lately, taking seat

On my accustomed bench of augury,
Whither all tribes of fowl after their kind
Alway resort, heard a strange noise of birds
Screaming with harsh and dissonant impetus ;
And was aware how each the other tore
With murderous talons ; for the whirr of wings
Rose manifest. Then feared I, and straight made trial
Of sacrifices on the altar-hearths
All blazing ; but, out of the offerings,
There sprang no flame ; only upon embers charred
Thick droppings melted off the thigh-pieces,
And heaved and sputtered, and the gall-bladders
Burst, and were lost, while from the folds of fat
The loosened thigh-bones fell. Such auguries,
Failing of presage through the unseemliness
Of holy rites, I gather from this lad,
Who is to me, as I to others, guide.
And this state-sickness comes by thy self-will ;
For all our hearths and altars are defiled
With prey of dogs and fowl, who have devoured
The dead unhappy son of Œdipus.
Therefore the Gods accept not of us now
Solemn peace-offering or burnt sacrifice,
Nor bird trills out a happy-boding note,
Gorged with the fatness of a slain man's blood.
This, then, my son, consider ; that to err
From the right path is common to mankind ;
But having erred, that mortal is no more
Losel or fool, who medicines the ill
Wherein he fell, and stands not obstinate.
Conceit of will savours of emptiness.
Give place, then, in the presence of the dead.
Wound not the life that's perished. Where's thy valour
In slaying o'er the slain ? Well I advise,

   Meaning thee well ; 'tis pleasantest to learn
   Of good advisers, when their words bring gain.

CREON. Old man, ye all, like archers at a mark,
   Are loosing shafts at me ; I am not spared
   Even your soothsayers' practice ; by whose tribe
   Long since have I been made as merchandize,
   And bought, and sold. Gather your gains at will !
   Market your Sardian silver, Indian gold !
   That man ye shall not cover with a tomb ;
   Not though the eagle ministers of Jove
   To Jove's own throne should bear their prey of him,
   Not even for horror at such sacrilege
   Will I permit his burial. This I know ;
   There is no power in any man to touch
   The Gods with sacrilege ; but foul the falls
   Which men right cunning fall, Tiresias—
   Old man, I say—when for the sake of gain
   They speak foul treason with a fair outside.

TIRESIAS. Alas, does no man know, does no man think—

CREON. What should one think ? What common saw is this ?

TIRESIAS. How far good counsel passes all things good ?

CREON. So far, I think, folly's the worst of harm !

TIRESIAS. That is the infirmity that fills thy nature.

CREON. I care not to retort upon thee, seer.

TIRESIAS. Thou dost, thou say'st my oracles are false.

CREON. All the prophetic tribe are covetous.

TIRESIAS. And that of kings fond of disgraceful gain.

CREON. Know'st thou of whom thou speak'st ? I am thy lord.

TIRESIAS. Yea, thou hast saved the state ; I gave it thee.

CREON. Thou art a wise seer, but in love with wrong.

TIRESIAS. Thou wilt impel me to give utterance
   To my still dormant prescience.

CREON.   Say on ;
   Only beware thou do not speak for gain.

TIRESIAS.   For gain of thine, methinks, I do not speak.
CREON.   Thou shalt not trade upon my wits, be sure.
TIRESIAS.   And be thou sure of this ; thou shalt not tell
        Many more turns of the sun's chariot-wheel,
        Ere thou shalt render satisfaction, one
        From thy own loins in payment, dead for dead,
        For that thou hast made Life join hands with Death,
        And sent a living soul unworthily
        To dwell within a tomb, and keep'st a corpse
        Here, from the presence of the Powers beneath,
        Not for thy rights or any God's above,
        But lawlessly in their despite usurped,
        Unhallowed, disappointed, uninterred ;
        Wherefore the late-avenging punishers,
        Furies, from Death and Heaven, lay wait for thee,
        To take thee in the evil of thine own hands.
        Look to it, whether I be bribed who speak ;
        For as to that, with no great wear of time,
        Men's, women's wails to thine own house shall answer.
        Also all cities rise in enmity,
        To the strown relics of whose citizens
        None pays due hallowing, save beasts of prey,
        Dogs, or some fowl, whose pinions to their gates—
        Yea, to each hearth—bear taint defiling them.
        Such bolts, in wrath, since thou dar'st anger me,
        I loosen at thy bosom, archer-like,
        Sure-aimed, whose burning smart thou shalt not shun.
        Lead me away, boy, to my own home again ;
        And let him vent his spleen on younger men,
        And learn to keep a tongue more gentle, and
        A brain more sober, than he carries now.

                          [*Exeunt* TIRESIAS *and Boy.*

1 SENATOR.   The seer is gone, my lord, denouncing woe ;
    And from the day my old hairs began to indue
    Their white for black, we have known him for a watch
    Who never barked to warn the state in vain.

CREON.   I know it too ; and I am ill at ease ;
    'Tis bitter to submit ; but Até's[1] hand
    Smites bitterly on the spirit that abides her.

1 SENATOR.   Creon Menœceus' son, be wise at need !

CREON.   What should I do ?   speak, I will hearken.

1 SENATOR.   Go,
    Set free the maiden from the vault, and build
    A tomb for that dead outcast.

CREON.   You approve it ?
    You deem that I should yield ?

1 SENATOR.   Sir, with all speed.
    Swift-footed come calamities from Heaven
    To cut off the perverse.

CREON.   O God, 'tis hard !
    But I quit heart, and yield ; I cannot fight
    At odds with destiny.

1 SENATOR.   Up then, to work !
    Commit it not to others !

CREON.   I am gone
    Upon the instant.   Quickly, quickly, men,
    You and your fellows, get you, axe in hand,
    Up to the place, there, yonder ; and because
    I am thus minded, other than before,
    I who did bind her will be there to loose ;
    For it misgives me it is best to keep
    The old appointed laws, all our life long.

           [*Exeunt* CREON *and Attendants.*

---

[1] Goddess of retribution.

CHORUS.

I. 1.

Thou by many names addrest,
Child of Zeus loud-thundering,
Glory of a Theban maid, [1]
Who unbidden wanderest
    Fair Italia's King, [2]
And art lord in each deep glade
Whither all men seek to her,
Eleusinian Demeter ; [3]
Bacchus, who by soft-flowing waters
Of Ismenus [4] habitest
Theba, mother of Bacchant daughters,
With the savage Dragon's stock,

I. 2.

Thee the lurid wild-fire meets
O'er the double-crested rock,
Where Corycian [5] Nymphs arow
Bacchic-wise ascending go,
    Thee Castalia's [6] rill ;
Thee the ivy-covered capes
Usher forth of Nysa's hill, [7]

---

[1] Bacchus (Dionysus) was the son of Zeus and the Theban Semele, who died of the lightning flashes emanating from her divine lover.
[2] Because of the many grapevines there (?).
[3] Goddess of grain with a sanctuary at Eleusis, outside Athens.
[4] Local river.
[5] Named for a cave on Mount Parnassus, near Delphi.
[6] A spring on Parnassus.
[7] In Phocis, where Dionysus grew up.

And the shore with green of grapes
Clustering, where the hymn to thee
Rises up immortally,
Visitant in Theban Streets,
" Evoe, O Evoe ! "[1]

II. 1.

Wherefore, seeing thy City thus—
City far above all other
Dear to thee, and her, thy mother
Lightning-slain—by sickness grievous
Holden fast in all her gates,
Come with quickness to relieve us,
By the slopes of Parnasus,
   Or the roaring straits.

II. 2.

Hail to thee, the first advancing
In the stars' fire-breathing chorus !
Leader of the nightly strain,
Boy and son of Zeus and King !
Manifest thyself before us
With thy frenzied Thyiad[2] train,
Who their lord Iacchus[3] dancing
   Praise, and all night sing.

Enter a MESSENGER.

---

[1] Bacchic chant.
[2] Female devotees..
[3] Bacchus.

MESSENGER. You citizens who dwell beside the roof
    Of Cadmus and Amphion,[1] there is no sort
    Of human life that I could ever praise,
    Or could dispraise, as constant ; Fortune still
    Raising and Fortune overthrowing still
    The happy and the unhappy ; and none can read
    What is set down for mortals. Creon, methought
    Was enviable erewhile, when he preserved
    This land of Cadmus from its enemies,
    And took the country's absolute monarchy,
    And ruled it, flourishing with a noble growth
    From his own seed ; and now, he has lost all.
    For when men forfeit all their joys in life,
    One in that case I do not count alive,
    But deem of him as of some animate corse.
    Pile now great riches, if thou wilt, at home ;
    Wear thou the living semblance of a king ;
    An if delight be lacking, all the rest
    I would not purchase, as compared with joy,
    From any, for the shadow of a shade.

1 SENATOR. What new affliction to the royal stock
    Com'st thou to tell ?

MESSENGER.   Death is upon them—death
    Caused by the living.

1 SENATOR.   And who is the slayer ?
    Speak ! who the victim ?

MESSENGER.   Hæmon is no more ;
    His life-blood spilt, and by no stranger's hand.

1 SENATOR. What, by his father's, or his own ?

MESSENGER.   Self-slaughtered ;
    Wroth with his father for the maiden slain.

1 SENATOR. Prophet ! how strictly is thy word come true !

---

[1] Amphion, husband of Niobe, and a builder of Thebes.

MESSENGER.   Look to the future, for these things are so.
1 SENATOR.   And I behold the poor Eurydice
   Come to us from the palace, Creon's wife ;
   Either of chance, or hearing her son's name.

Enter EURYDICE.

EURYDICE.   O all you citizens, I heard the sound
   Of your discourse, as I approached the gates,
   Meaning to bring my prayers before the face
   Of Pallas ; even as I undid the bolts,
   And set the door ajar, a voice of woe
   To my own household pierces through my ears ;
   And I sink backward on my handmaidens
   Afaint for terror ; but whate'er the tale,
   Tell it again ; I am no novice, I,
   In misery, that hearken.
MESSENGER.   Dear my mistress,
   I saw, and I will speak, and will let slip
   No syllable of the truth.   Why should we soothe
   Your ears with stories, only to appear
   Liars thereafter ? Truth is alway right.
   —I followed in attendance on your lord,
   To the flat hill-top, where despitefully
   Was lying yet, harried by dogs, the body
   Of Polynices.   Pluto's name, and hers,
   The wayside goddess,[1] we invoked, to stay
   Their anger and be favourable ; and him
   We washed with pure lustration, and consumed
   On fresh-lopped branches the remains of him,
   And piled a monument of natal earth
   High over all ; thence to the maiden's cell,
   Chamber of death, with bridal couch of stone,

---

[1] Hecate, an underworld goddess.

We made as if to enter.   But afar
One fellow hears a loud uplifted wail
Fill all the unhallowed precinct ; comes, and tells
His master, Creon ; the uncertain sound
Of piteous crying, as he draws more nigh,
Comes round him, and he utters, groaning loud,
A lamentable plaint ; " Me miserable !
Was I a prophet ? Is this path I tread
The unhappiest of all ways I ever went ?
My son's voice thrills my ear.   What ho, my guard !
Run quickly thither to the tomb where stones
Have been dragged down to make an opening,
Go in and look, whether I really hear
The voice of Hæmon, or am duped by Heaven.
Quickly, at our distracted lord's command,
We looked : and in the tomb's inmost recess
Found we her, as she had been hanged by the neck,
Fast in a strip-like loop of linen ; and him
Laid by her, clasping her about the waist,
Mourning his wedlock severed in the grave,
And his sire's deeds, and his ill-fated bride.
He, when he sees them, with a terrible cry
Goes in towards him, calling out aloud
" Ah miserable, what hast thou done ? what mind
Hadst thou ? by what misfortune art thou crazed ?
Come out, my son,—suppliant I ask of thee ! "
But with fierce aspect the youth glared at him ;
Spat in his face ; answered him not a word ;
Grasped at the crossed hilts of his sword and drew it,
And—for the father started forth in flight—
Missed him ! then, angered with himself, poor fool,
There as he stood he flung himself along
Upon the sword-point firmly planted in
The middle of his breast, and, conscious yet,

Clings to the maid, clasped in his failing arms,
And gasping, sends forth on the pallid cheek
Fast welling drops of blood : So lies he, dead,
With his arms round the dead ; there, in the grave
His bridal rite is full ; his misery
Is witness to mankind what worst of woe
The lack of counsel brings a man to know !

[*Exit* EURYDICE.

1 SENATOR.   What do you make of this ? The woman's gone
Back, and without one word, of good or bad !
MESSENGER.   I marvel too ; and yet I am in hope
She would not choose, hearing her son's sad fate,
In public to begin her keening-cry ;
But rather to her handmaids in the house
Dictate the mourning for a private pain.
She is not ignorant of self-control,
That she should err.
1 SENATOR.   I know not ; but on me
Weigh heavily both silence over-much,
And loud complaint in vain.
MESSENGER.   Well, we shall know it,
If she hide aught within a troubled heart
Even to suppression of its utterance,
If we approach the house.   Yes, you say truly,
It does weigh heavy, silence over-much.

[*Exit*.

CHORUS.

Lo now, Creon himself draws near us,
Clasping a record
Manifest, if we sin not, saying it,
Of ruin unwrought by the hands of others,
    But fore-caused by his own self-will.

Enter CREON, *attended, with the body of* HÆMON.

I. 1.

CREON.   O sins of a mind
                 That is minded to stray !
              Mighty to bind
                 And almighty to slay !
      Behold us, kin slayers and slain, O ye who stand by the
         way !

              Ah, newness of death !
                 O my fruitless design !
              New to life's breath,
                 O son that wert mine,
      Ah, ah, thou art dead, thou art sped, for a fault that was
         mine, not thine !

1 SENATOR.   Ah, how thou seem'st to see the truth, too late !
CREON.   Ah yes, I have learnt, I know my wretchedness !

II. 1.

              Heaviness hath o'ertaken me
                 And mine head the rod ;
              The roughness hath shaken me
                 Of the paths I trod ;
      Woe is me ! my delight is brought low, cast under the feet
         of a God !

              Woe for man's labours that are profitless !

Re-enter the MESSENGER.

MESSENGER.   O master, now thou hast and hast in store
                 Of sorrows ; one thou bearest in thine arms,

And one at home thou seemest to be come
Merely to witness.

CREON.   And what more of sorrow,
Or what more sorrowful, is yet behind ?

MESSENGER.   Thy wife, the mother—mother of the dead—
Is, by a blow just fallen, haplessly slain.

I. 2.

CREON.   O hard to appease thee,
                Haven of Death,
                How should it please thee
                To end this breath ?
O herald of heavy news, what is this thy mouth uttereth ?

                O man, why slayest thou
                A man that is slain ?
                Alas, how sayest thou
                Anew and again
That the slaying of a woman is added to slaying—a pain to
        a pain ?

MESSENGER.   See for thyself ; the palace doors unclose.

The Altar is disclosed, with the dead body of EURYDICE.

CREON.   Woe is me again, for this new sorrow I see.

II. 2.

                What deed is not done ?
                What tale is not told ?
                Thy body, O son,
                These arms enfold—

> Dead—wretch that I am !   Dead, too, is the face these eyes
>   behold.
>
>   Ah, child, for thy poor mother !   ah for thee !

MESSENGER.   She with a sharp-edged dagger in her heart
              Lies at the altar ; and her darkened lids
              Close on her wailing for the glorious lot
              Of Megareus,[1] who died before, and next
              For his, and last, upon her summoning
              Evil to fall on thee, the child-slayer !

III. 1.

CREON.   Alas, I faint for dread !
                      Is there none will deal
                    A thrust that shall lay me dead
                      With the two-edged steel ?
                    Ah woe is me !
                    I am all whelmed in utter misery !

MESSENGER.   It may be so ; thou art arraigned of her
              Who here lies dead, for the occasion thou
              Hast wrought for Destiny on her, and him.
1 SENATOR.   In what way did she slay herself and die ?
MESSENGER.   Soon as she heard the raising of the wail
              For her son's death, she stabbed herself to the heart.

IV. 1.

CREON.   Woe is me ! to none else can they lay it,
              This guilt, but to me !

---

[1] Her husband before Creon (?).

I, I was the slayer, I say it,
    Unhappy, of thee !
O bear me, haste ye, spare not,
    To the ends of earth,
More nothing than they who were not
    In the hour of birth !

1 SENATOR.   Thou counsellest well—if anything be well
        To follow, in calamity ; the ills
        Lying in our path, soonest o'erpast, were best.

III. 2.

CREON.   Come, thou most welcome Fate,
                    Appear, O come ;
                Bring my days' final date,
                    Fill up their sum !
                Come quick, I pray ;
                Let me not look upon another day !

1 SENATOR.   This for to-morrow ; we must take some thought
        On-that which lies before us ; for these griefs,
        They are their care on whom the care has fallen.
CREON.   I did but join your prayer for our desire.
1 SENATOR.   Pray thou for nothing more ; there is no respite
        To mortals from the ills of destiny.

IV. 2.

CREON.   Lead me forth, cast me out, no other
                Than a man undone ;
            Who did slay, unwitting, thy mother
                And thee, my son !

I turn me I know not where
   For my plans ill-sped,
And a doom that is heavy to bear
   Is come down on my head.

                   [*Exit* CREON, *attended*.

CHORUS.

Wisdom first for a man's well-being
Maketh, of all things.   Heaven's insistence
Nothing allows of man's irreverence ;
And great blows great speeches avenging,
   Dealt on a boaster,
Teach men wisdom in age, at last.

                   [*Exeunt omnes*.